HAMSTER-SAURUS REX

GETS CRUSHED

SAURUS REX

GETS CRUSHED

HARPER
An Imprint of HarperCollinsPublishers

SPECTMEN

ALSO BY TOM O'DONNELL

ISBN 978-0-06-237758-6

Typography by Joe Merkel
17 18 19 20 21   PC/LSCH   10 9 8 7 6 5 4 3 2 1
❖
First Edition

For Kieran, Ronan, Amelia, and Duke
—T.O.D.
For Morgan and McKenzie
—T.M.

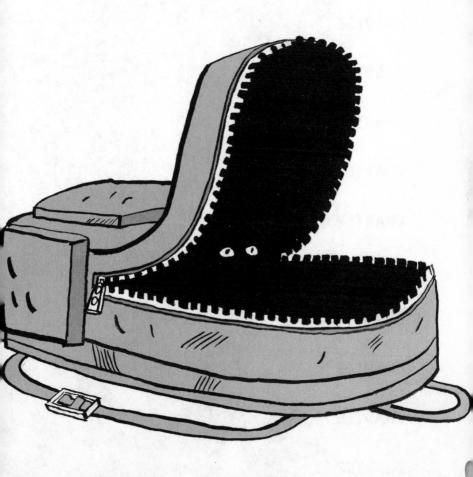

CONTENTS

CHAPTER 1

"...AND BY FINISHING that quintuple cheeseburger, he impressed all the other Founding Fathers," said Mr. Copeland. "And John Adams would ever after be known as John 'Quintuple Cheeseburger' Adams—or John 'Quincy' Adams for short!"

We stared back at him in silence. He sighed.

"Okay, that was a test," said Mr. Copeland. "None of you are listening to me, are you?"

I knew I wasn't. Instead I was drawing a picture of Hamstersaurus Rex competing in the Cyber Pole Vault at the 3016 Olympics. Unfortunately, his left eye was looking a bit wonky. I erased it and glanced toward the hamster cage in the back of the room for reference. Of course, the cage was empty. I kept forgetting Hamstersaurus Rex wasn't there.

"I just talked for five minutes about how everyone in the 1700s had gills!" said Mr. Copeland. "C'mon, Martha. I expect this from the other kids, but you?"

"Apologies, Mr. Copeland," said Martha Cherie, sixth-grade Hamster Monitor and Horace Hotwater Middle School's all-time GPA leader. "I'm a bit distracted. You see, I'm ever so excited for the big announcement I'm about to make! Speaking of which: May I address the class?"

Mr. Copeland gritted his teeth. "How would you feel if I came down to one of your clubs or dance lessons or extracurricular activities and just started randomly teaching history?!"

"That would be *amazing*," said Martha.

"Okay, fine, you called my bluff," said Mr. Copeland. "Just get on with it." He plopped down in his chair and cracked open one of his spy novels.

"Thank you, Arnold." Martha stood and smiled. "Greetings, dear classmates!"

"Greetings, Martha," we mumbled in unison. I turned to Dylan D'Amato, my best friend, to exchange an eye roll. But Dylan was staring at the floor, biting her nails. Weird.

"For one month," said Martha, "our class has languished, hamsterless. Our PETCATRAZ Pro™ has stood empty, but perhaps not as empty as our hearts. I am proud to announce that all of that changes today." Martha took a small mesh carrying case from under her desk. "Allow me to introduce your collective new best friend: Cartimandua!"

Martha unzipped the case and pulled out a splotchy brown hamster. There were a few claps scattered around the room. The hamster stared at the wall. It didn't blink.

Martha continued: "In the past, having a class pet has been marked by unfortunate escapes, kidnappings, and hamster-related property damage. But in Cartimandua we finally have a safe and appropriate animal companion. Her care will be an easy task for our seasoned Hamster Monitor team. In fact, let's hear it for the Hamster Monitors! Sam, Dylan, why don't we all take a bow?"

3

"Huh?" said Dylan, startled.

"You mean literally?" I said.

Martha nodded.

"Nah, I think I'm okay," I said. I stayed seated.

"Suit yourselves." Martha shrugged, then bowed alone. "At this time, I will open the floor for a brief Q and A about Cartimandua. Does anyone have any questions?"

"Yeah—how do you say the new hamster's name?" said Omar Powell. "I'm not getting it. Car . . . Carbonara?"

"Cartographia?" said Tina Gomez.

"Carpet-tarantula!" said Jared Kopernik.

"Car-tuh-MAN-doo-uh," said Martha, drawing out the syllables. "Like the ancient Celtic queen."

"Ah. Of course. *Like the ancient Celtic queen*," said Omar, shaking his head.

"Question," said Julie Bailey. "Is it too late to give this hamster a new name? Like a better one than the one you gave her?"

"Yes, it's too late," said Martha, scowling a little.

"Follow-up," said Julie. "Is it too late to get a new hamster?"

"Yes," said Martha, scowling more. "Anyone else?"

"Carbohydrate looks kind of zoned out," said Jimmy Choi. "Why doesn't she do anything?"

There was a chorus of general agreement from the other kids.

"Well, I'm glad you asked, Jimmy," said Martha. "In addition to zoning out and sometimes twitching, she also poops every three hours—like clockwork—*exactly* what a normal, healthy hamster is supposed to!"

"But Hamstersaurus Rex did all kinds of awesome stuff," said Jimmy. "He could smash things!"

"Right," said Martha, "but that was—"

"And he could walk around on his hind legs!" cried Caroline Moody. "And he ate *sometimes foods, all the time!*"

"Sure," said Martha. "It obviously goes without saying: we all love Ham—"

"And occasionally," said Tina, "we thought *maybe* he was evil and then he turned out *not* to be evil and that was *very* exciting!"

"Okay," said Martha, "but when you think

about it, was that really such a good—"

"He was almost better than snails," said Wilbur Weber.

"I agree, but—"

"Hamstersaurus Rex was a lovable rogue who taught us all the value of friendship!" cried Jared, pounding his fist on his desk.

The classroom broke out into applause. I had to smile a little. It felt good that everybody loved Hammie again.

"Well, Hamstersaurus Rex is gone and now we have Cartimandua!" snapped Martha. "And for the record, all that 'awesome stuff' he did—it nearly got him killed on multiple occasions. That's why our new hamster isn't going to eat junk food or break anything or even leave her cage, because we know from experience that it's far, *far* too dangerous. So, in conclusion, I hope we can all come to appreciate Cartimandua for who she is, and not constantly compare her to any former classroom hamsters."

"Eh," said Tina, "I hope you're not offended, but I just kind of feel like this new hamster,

Capoeira, is maybe just a little, *teensy* bit . . . wildly disappointing."

Martha was at a loss for words. She looked deflated. The big introduction had not gone as planned. I felt like I had to say something.

"Hey, you know, I happen to think Cartimandua's pretty cool," I said. "And you did an awesome job picking her out, Martha. Right, Dylan?"

"Oh," said Dylan, fidgeting with a piece of loose-leaf paper. "Yep. Uh-huh."

"Thank you, Sam. Thank you, Dylan," said Martha. She bowed again.

The bell for lunch rang and we all stood up from our desks. I beelined for the door, hoping to beat the crowd, but Tina Gomez flung herself in my path. I swallowed.

"Any updates on my missing pencil eraser?" asked Tina.

"Oooh. Well, we're, ah, pursuing various leads," I said, tapping my notebook.

Three days before, Tina Gomez had lost an eraser, and she was looking to me to find it for her. Honestly, I had no idea where the eraser was. My case notes (*pink, rubbery, black market for erasers???, erasers and pencils . . . natural enemies? Hmmm,* and *soooo hungry*) didn't make a ton of sense.

"Sam, that eraser had extreme sentimental value," said Tina. "I just can't handle the stress of not knowing where it is."

"I almost hate to suggest this," I said, "but erasers do cost, like, twenty-five cents. What if you, um, bought a new one?"

"No! It was irreplaceable!" said Tina, grabbing me by the collar. "Irreplaceable!"

"Right, sure, of course," I said.

"'Sup, Sam," said Drew McCoy, butting in, "have you figured out who stole my *Legend of Max Stomper* #338 gold-foil variant cover right out of my locker?"

"We're working on it," I said. "Making a lot of progress."

"Sam, did you solve my case yet?" said Dwight Feinberg, elbowing in. "The Case of Dwight Feinberg's Missing Instant Camera!"

"We have leads!" I cried. "Awesome leads! Just the best leads!" A crowd was starting to form around me. It was entirely composed of kids whose "cases" I'd taken on but hadn't yet solved. After recent (giant-squirrel-related) events, I had become known around school as a kid who could solve problems. But the thing about problems is that everybody's got them. It's possible that I had stretched myself a little thin. I was an ace detective, but full disclosure: I had yet to solve a single case.

"Sam, my eraser?" said Tina, nudging back to the front.

"Maybe the ghost took it," said Jared, before I could reply.

Tina looked horrified. "Is that one of your leads, Sam?"

"What? No! What? Ghost?" I said. "Jared, ghosts aren't real. And if they were, they wouldn't steal erasers, would they?"

"I know *most* ghosts aren't real," said Jared, "but this one totally is. It's the ghost of Horace Hotwater himself. He haunts these halls looking for revenge. I've seen some pretty weird stuff."

"You *are* some pretty weird stuff," I said.

"Come to think of it, I saw something strange,

too," said Julie. "The other day I was alone in the library and suddenly a door slammed all on its own."

"That was the wind," I said.

"Or was it?" said Jared.

"How could it be the ghost of Horace Hotwater?" I said. "The man died a hundred years ago and this school was built in 2002."

"Or was it?" said Jared.

"You can't just keep saying 'Or was it?' as a response to everything!" I said.

"Or was it?" said Jared.

"Look, your pencil eraser will be found," I said, ignoring Jared. "All your cases will be solved. We promise."

Tina grinned. "You keep saying 'we.' You're talking about you and Hamstersaurus Rex, right? You know where he is!"

"Hey, come on," I said. "We all know Hamstersaurus Rex is gone. Martha got us a new hamster and everything."

Drew grinned. "Sure he's gone."

"When you *don't* see him," said Dwight, "*don't*

tell him we all miss him."

"Won't do," I said, grinning despite myself.

My crowd of unsolved cases started to disperse, leaving one person remaining.

"Um, Sam, can I talk to you for a second?" said Dylan quietly. Normally confident and outspoken, she looked jittery. "Er, in private."

"Sure thing, Dylan," I said. "Hit me up at lunch. I just need to make a quick detour first."

She gave me a knowing nod. I headed up the stairs to the second floor. The hallway was lined with homemade posters that said things like, "We Miss You, Hamstersaurus Rex!" and "Come Back Soon, Hamster Hero of Horace Hotwater!" I opened the door to Room 223b—better known as Meeting Club Headquarters—and nearly got knocked down by the hero himself.

"Oof! Okay! I'm—oof!—happy to see—oof!—you, too!" I said as Hammie Rex repeatedly head-butted me in the stomach. Affectionately.

I shut the door behind me. The little guy was secretly living in this converted broom closet that held the library's least-checked-out books, such as *Europe's Greatest Sneezes* and *The Complete User's Guide to Manila Folders*. I felt kind of guilty cooping him up all day with nothing to do. But considering all the weirdos and mutants and evil corporations out to get him, he was ultimately safer here. It was sort of like the Hamster Monitor Witness Relocation Program (or something).

"Got your lunch." I unzipped my backpack and pulled out nine pimento cheese sandwiches. Hamstersaurus Rex took a flying leap at his helpless pimento prey. I nearly lost an arm. "While you eat, maybe we can review our caseload," I said. Every good gumshoe needs a partner, and mine was three inches of pure dino-rodent crime-stopping power. As a joke, I called us Rex & Gibbs Detective Agency.

"R&G has got so many open cases I have no idea which one we should focus on. Tina's missing eraser?" I asked, flipping through my notebook. "Or Dwight's camera? I'm thinking maybe he left it on the bus. Dwight seems like a real bus-leaver to me . . ."

I trailed off when something wet dripped on my head. It was drool. I looked up to see that Hamstersaurus Rex was now hanging upside down by his dino-tail from the light fixture. The little guy looked loopy.

"Wow, you're going stir-crazy in here, aren't you?" I said. "Hey, I've got an idea! After school, I'll take you to meet Martha's new hamster. That'll be fun, right? A new friend! Just hang tight for a couple more hours. No pun intended."

I left him dangling and made my way to the cafeteria for lunch. I found Dylan sitting by herself, staring off into space and gnawing on her fingers.

"Want a little salt for those nails?" I said.

"Gah!" screamed Dylan, startled. "Don't sneak up on me like that!"

"Whoa, whoa, whoa," I said. "I didn't mean to scare you, pal."

"Sorry," said Dylan. "It's just—I think I maybe need your help with something."

"Ah," I said, "so you have a *case* for me?"

"Do *not* call it a 'case,'" said Dylan, sounding a bit more like her normal self.

"Well, Hammie and I are pretty slammed right now," I said, "but I want you to know I consider you a friend, so *maybe* I could get you on the waiting list. Talk to our assista—"

I ducked too slowly and a wadded-up napkin hit me in the face. This was the Dylan who'd been my best friend since preschool.

"Sam, this is serious," said Dylan. "The other day, after school, I was grabbing my duffel bag for disc golf practice and something super weird happened."

"Go on."

"So the Hotwater Discwhippers have these awesome new away jerseys that are metallic mauve with maroon piping."

"Mmm-hmm," I said, taking out my notebook and scribbling notes. "Mauve and maroon. Got it."

"And when I opened my bag, I saw my jersey,

like . . . *float* right out of my locker and down the hall toward the basement stairs," said Dylan.

"Okay," I said, still writing, "and after that, something 'weird' happened, you say?"

"Sam, it really freaked me out!" said Dylan. "I just want to know what's going on around here." She clearly didn't see anything funny about levitating athletic wear.

"Yeah, sure," I said. "Flying jersey. Hammie and I will look into it. Hey, maybe it was the ghost of Horace Hotwater?"

I expected Dylan to laugh. Instead she scowled at me.

"You smell like pimento cheese," she said.

"You think I don't know that?" I asked.

The rest of the day was a blur: badminton, hexagons, homonyms, and a new case from Jared Kopernik. He wanted me to prove that Bigfoot *was* real but that the yeti *wasn't*. Fantastic. After the final bell rang, I ran back up to Meeting Club HQ. I opened the door and Hamstersaurus Rex flew at my face.

"Agh! Okay!" I said as he jumped up and down

on top of my head. "Save some of that charm for your new hamster pal." I wrangled him into my shirt pocket.

Downstairs, I jiggled the doorknob to Mr. Copeland's room. The lock was still broken. I pulled out my copy PETCATRAZ Pro™ key and unlocked Cartimandua's hamster cage. She stared at me indifferently.

"Hi, Cartimandua, my name is Sam Gibbs," I said. "How's it going?"

Cartimandua twitched a whisker.

"Well, enough small talk. There's someone I'd really like you to meet," I said. "You're a hamster. He's a hamster . . . mostly. And frankly, he really needs to get out more. Between you and me, he's kind of going bonkers, stuck in that tiny broom closet all day. Maybe you two could, like, play together?"

I reached into my pocket and plopped Hammie down in the cage beside her.

"Cartimandua, Hamstersaurus Rex," I said. "Hamstersaurus Rex, Cartimandua."

Hamstersaurus Rex didn't move. He had

frozen still like a statue. Cartimandua glanced at him and then turned to stare at the wall with slightly more interest. They weren't exactly playing.

"C'mon, Hammie, don't be rude," I said as I shoved him toward her. He made a weird chirping noise. Nothing I'd ever heard before.

"Uh, he's normally lots of fun," I said. "The life of the party."

Cartimandua yawned.

"Go on, Hammie," I said. "Do something cool!"

Hamstersaurus Rex looked at me. He looked at Cartimandua. He looked at me. He took a single hesitant step in her direction and—FLUMP!—the little guy tripped over her water dish and fell flat on his face. The dish flipped onto Cartimandua, completely soaking her. She started loudly squeaking in dismay. Hamstersaurus Rex looked mortified.

"Whoops!" I said. I grabbed a handful of paper towels and began to blot her fur dry. "No need to panic! Just water!"

WHAM! Somewhere down the hall I heard a door slam shut. I paused my blotting.

"That's weird," I said. Mr. Grogan, the custodian, didn't usually slam doors. In fact, I'd heard him yell at more than one kid for doing it.

WHAM! I heard another slam. It sounded like a different door. Something didn't feel right. I collected Hammie Rex, who had gone virtually catatonic at this point.

"This was fun," I lied, "but we have to go investigate. We're ace detectives who are eventually going to solve a case. Sorry about the water. Enjoy, uh, staring at the wall. Bye!"

Hammie and I ducked out into the hallway.

"Okay, that didn't go very well," I said to Hamstersaurus Rex.

He gurgled.

The school appeared to be deserted. We walked the halls, listening, but didn't hear anything more. The noises were probably nothing. On the way back to my locker, I paused at the steps that led down to the basement. A strange feeling came over me, almost like the air was electrified right before a thunderstorm. The hairs on my arm were standing up. I looked at Hamstersaurus Rex. His little whiskers were vibrating.

"Maybe we should check out the basement," I said. "Just in case it's a ghost, which it totally isn't."

I had started toward the steps when I heard a loud rattling sound. I turned to see that a bulletin board (celebrating the fall honor roll) was shaking wildly. It started to slam itself against the wall, harder and harder. No one was moving it. *It* was moving it.

". . . Or maybe not," I said, quietly backing away from the stairs and the board. Hammie Rex whined.

Just then, the bulletin board swung up from the wall so that it was flat, like a table. It hung like that for a moment before it ripped itself free and spun through the air, straight at my head.

Dodging Dylan's balled-up napkin was good practice. This time I ducked fast enough. With an earsplitting crack, the bulletin board smashed against the wall behind me and shattered into splinters.

After that, there was an eerie silence.

After *that*, there were the distinct sounds of me running away in terror.

CHAPTER 2

"**S**o . . . I WAS looking into the matter we discussed," I said to Dylan the next day at lunch, "and, well, I may have seen something a *taaaad* weird."

Dylan glanced around to make sure none of the other kids in the cafeteria were listening. "Like what?" she whispered.

"Like, a bulletin board *may* have tried to kill me."

"That's what you call a 'taaaaad' weird?"

"Look, I spend most of my time feeding a mutant hamster cheese sandwiches. Everything is relative," I said. "And anyway, I'm sure there's a logical explanation. I just have no idea what it could possibly be."

"There *is* an explanation," said Dylan. "He knows you're my best friend. That's why he's targeting you now. To get to me."

"Dylan, I'm not sure bulletin boards have genders—"

"Not the bulletin board," said Dylan. "The ghost of Horace Hotwater." Her words hung ominously in the air.

"Setting aside the fact that ghosts don't exist," I said, "why would the ghost of the man who founded our town be haunting you specifically? Was Horace not a disc golf fan?"

Dylan took a deep breath. "Sam, I'm going to tell you something that I don't want you to repeat. It's a dark and shameful family secret. A hundred years ago, my great-great-grandfather Giuseppe D'Amato killed Horace Hotwater."

"Whoa, that's pretty exciting!" I said. "The most interesting Gibbs family story is the one about my uncle Burt accidentally eating a bug."

Dylan scowled at me.

"Did I say 'exciting'? I meant 'tragic,'" I said. "So how'd it happen? Was it a sword fight? Please tell me it was a tragic sword fight."

"It wasn't a sword fight," said Dylan. "It was much, much worse. Giuseppe had a restaurant here in Maple Bluffs. Horace Hotwater came in to order lunch and my great-great-grandfather served him a bowl of soup . . . *that he choked on!*"

I cocked my head. "You mean 'drowned in'?"

"No!" said Dylan. "Do you have any idea how much soup it would take to drown someone?"

"Not really," I admitted.

"Well, it's a lot. Anyway, this was a bowl of Giuseppe D'Amato's famous turtle soup, but I guess he accidentally left a piece of shell in or whatever, because something got lodged in Horace Hotwater's windpipe and, well . . ." Dylan pantomimed choking on soup.

"Sounds like a freak accident," I said. "Could've happened to anyone."

"Tell that to the restless soul of Horace Hotwater!" said Dylan, jabbing a finger into my chest. "Do you know what his last words were, right before he died? *I will have my revenge, D'Amato.*"

"How did he say something if he was choking?"

"Stop nitpicking!" cried Dylan.

"Sorry," I said.

"I've heard the story from my nana Rosa every Thanksgiving since I was born," said Dylan. "She says the moral is: always chew your soup. But I think there's a different moral, and it's that the D'Amatos have been cursed by the ghost of Horace Hotwater!"

"C'mon. It's been a hundred years," I said. "Why would this curse start now?"

"*Because* it's been a hundred years!" said Dylan. "Exactly! To the day! Look!"

She pointed to the school plaque in the caf-eteria commemorating the "pioneering spirit and visionary fashion sense of the great Horace Hotwater." (Apparently he always wore shorts, before that was acceptable.) Sure enough, his date of death was a hundred years ago this week.

Horace Hotwater

"Er, I'll admit that's a little spooky," I said. "But it's just a coincidence."

"A bulletin board threw itself at your head. Was that a coincidence, too?" said Dylan. "And it's even worse. My disc golf game has been in the toilet. My grades are slipping. My dad's company says they might be downsizing. My mom sprained her ankle in the garden. Both my brothers have chicken pox. Oh, and that away jersey that levitated down the hall of its own accord? It was really expensive. If Coach Weekes finds out I lost it, he's going to kill me!"

"Hmm. Then maybe *you* can haunt *him*," I said.

Dylan was not amused. Normally, she was rational and cool-headed. This was very unlike her. I wanted to help.

"Look, I don't know what's going on," I said, "but strange is the new normal around here. I'm pretty sure the center of it all is down in the school basement. I got a real weird vibe from that place. After school, Hamstersaurus Rex and I will investigate, and we can prove once and for all that—"

"Hey, everyone, look at me!" bellowed Wilbur Weber, roughly six inches from my head.

"Sure, Wilbur," I said, rubbing my finger in my ringing ear. "I may no longer be able to *hear* you, but I can definitely *look*."

Wilbur ignored my snark. "I just wanted to announce that today I'm having my birthday party and the whole sixth grade is invited!"

The other kids in the cafeteria gave an uncertain murmur. Wilbur wasn't exactly the coolest kid in school. All he ever talked about was his pet snails.

"Oh, I almost forgot to mention," yelled Wilbur, "it's happening right after school at RaddZone!"

The cafeteria erupted. Some kids high-fived each other. Others pumped their fists. One actually did a ridiculous little dance (okay, it was me). Even Dylan looked a tiny bit happier. That's because RaddZone was our town's premier indoor youth-entertainment complex: three floors of go-karts, laser tag, and video games. The place was amazing!

"Hey, sorry about the hearing-loss crack earlier, Wilbur," I said. "My ears are fine. Maybe even better than before! Happy birthday, buddy! Can't wait to see you on the air hockey rink! Is it expected that guests bring a gift, or . . ."

But Wilbur ignored me as he made his way through a crowd of congratulatory sixth graders giving him fist bumps and patting him on the back.

"That's odd," said Martha Cherie, putting her tray down next to Dylan's and mine. "Wilbur's birthday was in June."

"Shhhhh," I said. "That's like reminding Mr. Copeland he forgot to assign us homework."

"Mr. Copeland forgot to assign us homework?" said Martha, suddenly panicked.

"No!" I said. "My point is that if Wilbur doesn't know when his own birthday is, so what? Who are we to judge? Don't ruin this for us. It's Radd-Zone, Martha."

"It is RaddZone," added Dylan.

Martha shrugged. "Well, put me down for a 'Will Not Attend.' I have hip-hop French horn lessons this afternoon. You know, I frankly never saw the appeal of RaddZone. What, the purpose is simply to have fun?"

"Yes!" said Dylan and I, in unison.

"Well, that's not going to help anyone get into college," said Martha.

Maybe not, I thought, but it might just take everyone's mind off evil curses and deadly soup.

CHAPTER 3

AFTER LUNCH, I swung by Meeting Club HQ to check on Hamstersaurus Rex. I opened the door to find that his food—a pan of lasagna and a six-pound bag of brussels sprouts—was untouched. This was unprecedented. Hammie Rex lay on his back gazing up at a water stain on the ceiling. The little guy looked shell-shocked.

"What's the matter?" I said. "Does the lasagna taste weird? I know my mom can get get a little trigger-happy with the oregano."

He made a sound like the air being let out of a bike tire.

"Hmm. Well, you know how I said we were

going to investigate the mysterious evil in the school basement this afternoon? That got bumped to tomorrow. You and I are going to RaddZone! Yaaaay!"

He gave a very, very slow blink.

"Not quite the reaction I was hoping for," I said, scratching my chin. "You seem a little off today, buddy. Luckily, RaddZone is the funnest place on earth! They've got ball pits, and those basketball games where the ball never goes in the basket, and all the baked potatoes you can eat just sitting there under heat lamps! You're going to love it!"

He tried to burp but couldn't quite manage it.

"Something's up," I said. "Ever since I introduced you to Cartimandua—"

At the name, he made another strangled chirp and scurried under an overturned copy of *So You Want to Make a Sandwich, Ninth Edition*.

"Huh? Dude, you fought a killer python and a nine-foot squirrel. Don't tell me you're afraid of Cartimandua?"

Another weird chirp. I had no idea what was

going on. I'd never seen the little guy like this before. I looked around the room. My eyes fell on a dog-eared copy of 101 *Love Poems plus 37 Bonus Poems about Lawn Care*. Suddenly it all made sense.

"Oh no," I said. "You've got a crush on Cartimandua."

Hammie Rex peeked out from under the book. I could see it in his eyes. The little guy was smitten. I winced. There was no way around it: he'd obviously made a terrible first impression on Cartimandua.

"Well," I said, "you should keep in mind that there are plenty of *other* single hamsters out there . . ."

Hammie Rex moaned in anguish. I tried to shush him. He kept on moaning.

"Or maybe I could help you impress her and that would make you feel better!" I suggested.

He stopped moaning.

In gym class, I sidled up next to Martha near the badminton court.

"Hey, Martha, I'd like to know a little more about Cartimandua," I said.

"Did you read the handouts I gave you?" said Martha.

I hadn't. "Absolutely," I said. "Very informative stuff. But that was all about hamsters in general. I want to know about Cartimandua, the real Cartimandua. What are her hopes? Her dreams? What makes her tick?"

Martha paused. "She likes lettuce . . . in moderation. And sleeping." Martha was struggling a little. "When Cartimandua's awake, I feel like she really enjoys staring off into middle distance."

I glanced around to make sure no one was listening. "Well, imagine that, hypothetically, *someone* wanted to get to know her a little better because *someone* maybe has a massive crush on her."

Martha looked confused. Then she frowned. "I'd say *someone* ought to forget about it."

"But why?"

"Because *someone* is a magnet for trouble. That's why *someone* is secretly living in a broom closet, remember? And the less discreet *someone* is, the more trouble there will be."

"Martha, look in your heart," I said. "Give love a chance!"

"No, thank you," said Martha. "I'd prefer to give good judgment and practicality a chance." Then she jogged onto the court to play her match against Jimmy Choi.

"Come on! Be less reasonable!" I said. "Ugh!"

"What's the matter, Gibbs?" said Coach Weekes, ambling toward me. "You sound frustrated. Like you're not living up to one hundred percent of your potential."

"What?" I said. "No, no, it's just that a friend of mine is, uh, a little out of sorts right now over a personal matter. That's all."

"Sure, a 'friend,'" said Coach Weekes, doing the slowest, most exaggerated air quotes I'd ever seen. He smiled at me with pity.

"Coach, it's not me! Seriously, it's Ham—Never mind," I said. "Look, can we just talk about something else? Hey, crystals! You're really into crystals, right? Tell me about crystals!"

"Nah, I'm over crystals," said Coach Weekes. "Incense, too. I used to be searching for answers, Gibbs, but then I realized I had them all along. Right here." He tapped the side of his head.

"In your hat?" I said.

He placed a hand on my shoulder. "You know, when that gigantic mutated squirrel-beast was dangling me off that scoreboard, I experienced a lot of personal growth."

"Personal growth?"

"I realized that sometimes meditation and spiritual strength aren't quite enough to win at the game of life," said Weekes. "Occasionally, all of us need a little nudge to become a huge success. Like I am now. So from this day forward, I'm going to devote myself to helping your quote-unquote 'friend' achieve his personal goals by becoming his Success Coach. . . . Wow, 'Success Coach.' I *really* like the sound of that."

"I don't," I said.

"Success Coach's first rule," said Coach Weekes. "Get out of your comfort zone! Take a walk. Climb a mountain. Explore an undersea trench. Go to that hoity-toity restaurant you were always so intimidated by because they don't serve chicken nuggets to adults!"

"How would I explore an undersea trench?"

"Believe it and achieve it and probably rent a submarine!" said Coach Weekes, cuffing me on the back. "Success Coach!"

Taking any advice from Coach Weekes was like taking guitar lessons from a parking meter:

probably not helpful. Still, I had to admit I knew nothing about romance, much less *hamster* romance. Success Coach's first rule rattled around in my brain for the rest of the day. Maybe Hammie Rex *could* get out of his comfort zone (the school). Maybe he and Cartimandua could go somewhere together. Somewhere special. Like on a date. A hamster date, if you will. It suddenly struck me that Hammie and I were already headed somewhere special that very afternoon: RaddZone! What if I brought Cartimandua along, too? Of course, Martha didn't want Cartimandua out of her cage. But Martha wasn't going to be there, was she?

By the end of the day, I'd made up my mind. Hamstersaurus Rex and Cartimandua were going on an amazing hamster date to Radd-Zone. I swung by Meeting Club HQ after school and collected Hammie Rex. He was by turns reluctant and ecstatic. Eventually I managed to wrangle him into my shirt pocket, where he seemed to be continuously hyperventilating.

"Just be yourself!" I said. "But not too much like yourself."

School was practically empty now, eerily quiet with all the students gone. I crept back down to Mr. Copeland's classroom and ducked inside.

Inside her PETCATRAZ Pro™, Cartimandua was chewing on her foot. I unlocked the door.

"Hello again, Cartimandua! We're going on a cool adventure to a place that you're going to love! How does that sound?"

She drooled a little. Inside my pocket, Hammie Rex made a terrified wheezing noise.

"Okay, neat. I'm going to assume you're very excited." I scooped her up and tucked her into my other pocket.

Just then, I heard a noise. My heart ricocheted into my throat as I remembered the awful, eerie feeling I got just before the bulletin board launched itself at my head. I spun and saw nothing.

Then the doorknob jiggled. I swallowed. Was

there actually a chance the school was haunted by some vengeful spirit from beyond the grave? No way. And yet.

The door slowly creaked open . . .

CHAPTER 4

"**G**AAAAAH!" **SHRIEKED DYLAN** as she opened the door and saw me standing inside the darkened classroom.

"Aaaaargh!" I responded, startled by her reaction.

"Sam, *why* are you hiding in here in the dark?!" cried Dylan, slugging me in the arm. "You nearly scared me to death!"

"Well, why are you sneaking around the school after hours?" I said. "I thought you were a—"

"Ghost?" said Dylan.

"No," I said. "You just surprised me, okay."

"I only came back here because I accidentally

left my workout socks in my desk," said Dylan, grabbing them. "But now I think I need to lie down."

"I came to get Cartimandua because she and Hamstersaurus Rex are going on a hamster date."

"A hamster date?" said Dylan, cocking her head. "Sam, you make weird choices."

"Can't argue with that," I said. "Anyway, we're all going to Wilbur's birthday party at RaddZone."

"What about your plan to investigate the . . ." Dylan's voice dropped to a whisper, and she glanced over her shoulder. ". . . *the creepy haunted basement?*"

"Oh, that? Hammie and I are going to knock that out tomorrow, easy-peasy," I said. "Look, even if it is some sort of evil undead poltergeist—which it's certainly not—think about it this way: Horace Hotwater has been dead for a hundred years, right? The guy can be dead another day."

"I don't know, Sam," said Dylan with a shiver. "I'm getting a really bad vibe. Something very creepy is going on at this school."

"Sure: math class!" I said. "Look, you know what would really take your mind off 'the curse'? Some go-karts and a loaded baked potato at the most awesome place in town, possibly the world."

"Hmm. I'm not exactly in the mood for a party," said Dylan.

"If not a party, how about a jamboree?" I said with a grin. "Perhaps of the Country Gopher Family variety."

RaddZone's special musical/variety show was called the Country Gopher Family Jamboree. An animatronic family of hillbilly gophers (Gomer, Big Virgil, Sweetie Pie, Aunt Ellie Mae, Dweasel, Leisl, and Grumpy Grampy) played jug band instruments and told corny jokes and said "aw shucks" and "tarnation" for eleven minutes every half hour. As long as Dylan and I had been friends, we'd considered the Country Gopher Family Jamboree to be the most ridiculous, hilarious thing in the world.

Dylan cracked a smile. "Remember last time we were there?"

"Gomer Gopher's tail fell off right in the middle of his drum solo!" I said, giggling.

"I bet you ten official RaddZone prize tickets that nobody's even bothered to reattach it."

"Ten prize tickets? That's a value of almost seven cents!" I said. "You're on!"

That settled it. We were going to RaddZone. With a hamster in each pocket and my best friend at my side, I set a course for fun. Well, Dylan's dad set a course. In his hybrid SUV.

The nondescript strip mall that housed Radd-Zone gave no clue what lay inside. But sandwiched between a Coat Barn and a Harry's Health Food Hut, was an earthly paradise for sixth graders. As we pulled over to the curb, I felt my pulse quicken.

"You know, back in my day, I set the high score on Ms. Super Plunger Jr. at the Laundromat down the block," said Mr. D'Amato. "Maybe I ought to come inside and show you kids how it's done." He cracked his knuckles.

"That's cool, Dad," said Dylan. "I'm not sure they have Ms. Super Plunger Jr. at RaddZone. Maybe check a museum?"

"Or under one of the pyramids," I offered.

"Ha-ha," said Mr. D'Amato. "Your generation is fooled by fancy graphics and Wi-Fi capability, but video games peaked thirty-three years ago. At my neighborhood Laundromat. FRA lives!"

"Huh?" said Dylan.

"Ms. Super Plunger Jr. only let me put in three letters when I got the high score," said Mr. D'Amato with a shrug. "Not enough room for Frank."

Dylan and I got out of the car and walked through the double doors emblazoned with the grinning face of Gomer Gopher, RaddZone's cartoon mascot. Inside was a space roughly the size

of an airplane hangar: an open floor plan housing three floors of arcade games, batting cages, an indoor go-cart track, and a laser tag arena. High above everything towered Mount Putta-Putta, the complex's mini-golf course, styled as a fake Hawaiian volcano. A cloud of dry ice puffed out of its mighty crater. I almost teared up every time I walked into RaddZone. Somehow it felt like . . . coming home.

Wilbur's party was already in full swing. His parents must have rented out the entire place, because I recognized everyone there from school. Jimmy Choi was locked in a tense Skee-Ball shoot-out with Caroline Moody. Drew McCoy was simultaneously eating two corn dogs while ordering a third. Tina Gomez handed a wad of tickets to the hulking teen at the prize counter. She didn't have enough for any of the Country Gopher Family masks, so she settled for a pencil eraser that said "RaddZone" on it. I guess her old one wasn't irreplaceable after all.

"Mmm. The smell of nacho cheese; the sound of tokens disappearing into coin slots forever; the slightly sticky carpet beneath your feet," I said to Dylan. "Feeling any better yet?"

"Maybe a little," said Dylan. "I think I need to beat you at air hockey a couple dozen times to take the edge off."

"You got it," I said. "Hang on, there's something I need to do first." I'd almost forgotten that my pockets were full of rodents who needed a little nudge toward romance. The hamster date!

I sidled up to the snack bar.

"Um, pardon me, ma'am," I said to the teenage girl behind the counter. "What's your most romantic food item?"

"Dunno. RaddSpudd?" She shrugged. "That's what we call a loaded baked potato."

"Oh, I *know* what a RaddSpudd is," I said, plunking some money down. "One, please. Extra romantic!"

She sighed and took my money. As I waited for my order, I made a mental checklist of all the arcade games I was going to play while I was here: Shark Punch definitely; Alien Autopsy: Turbo obviously; Tiny Wizards IV for sure; the

Muscle Meter where you hit the sensor with a big mallet and it tested your strength . . . maybe? I usually scored a "Pasta Arms," but maybe today was the day I could hit it hard enough to be a "Jumbo Shrimp." Across the snack bar, I noticed a girl standing alone beside the soft-serve machine. She had dyed purple hair and wore a T-shirt with an image on it that looked like a smiley face with no eyes. I didn't recognize her, yet she was somehow . . . familiar. She definitely didn't go to Horace Hotwater Middle School (no one with purple hair did). Maybe Wilbur had other friends? I was looking at the floor when I realized that Purple Hair was staring right back at me. I suddenly remembered where I'd seen that odd smiley design before. It was the SmilesCorp logo! I looked back up, but Purple Hair had vanished. Creepy.

"Here," said the snack bar girl, startling me. She handed me my RaddSpudd. "I tried to shape the chili glob into a heart, but it kind of ended up looking more like a lung. Sorry."

I found a deserted corner on the second floor with a dusty Love Tester machine that, if I had to guess, no one had put a token into in fifteen years. Nearby was a jukebox. I changed four dollars into tokens and then put on as many songs with "Love" in the title as I could afford.

"All right, you two hamster kids!" I said, taking Cartimandua and Hamstersaurus Rex out of my pockets. "Have fun, and don't let anybody see you! Neither one of you is *technically* supposed to be here. We don't want the employees to mistake you for an infestation."

Hammie Rex's eyes were as big as saucers. He stared at me like he was going to die. Cartimandua yawned, rolled over, and went to sleep.

"When she wakes up from the nap, you guys are going to have so much fun," I said. "RaddZone is a very romantic place! True story: this is where I first fell in love with nachos."

I poked out my index finger to give Hamster-saurus Rex the world's smallest high five. For the first time ever, the little guy left me hanging.

"Whatever," I said, shaking my head. "Enjoy your loaded baked potato. I'll be back in a couple of hours."

I found Dylan at the air hockey tables.

"Hello, my friend," said Dylan, twirling the puck on her finger. "Ready to become a human sacrifice to the mighty gods of miniature table sports?" She seemed to be back to her old cocky, competitive self.

Dylan is way better than I am at air hockey (and all sports and games, and most, you know, *things* in life generally) but somehow I beat her at air hockey three times in a row. The first two matches I was playing my best. The third one I intended to lose but I somehow still won after Dylan scored on her own goal three times. She was really off her game.

"Sorry," I said after winning that third match.

"I don't know what's happened to me," said Dylan, looking at her hands in disgust. "I think it's the curse of Horace Hotwater."

"Come on," I said. "You're telling me that a vengeful pioneer ghost is taking the time to mess with your air hockey game? Whatever happened to bleeding walls and making people's heads spin around?"

"You're right," said Dylan with a nervous laugh. "I'm being ridiculous."

We played Skee-Ball. I beat her. We played ring toss. I beat her. We played that game where you shoot the little ducks with an air rifle. Her performance was, er, lacking.

"I didn't hit a single duck," said Dylan.

"Maybe that's a good thing," I said. "Why are we shooting at them, anyway? What did they ever do to us? The cycle of violence needs to stop!"

"It's the curse," whispered Dylan. "It has to be."

"You don't know that," I said. "You're just having an off day."

"Sam, I'm losing at things that require focus and hand-eye coordination to *you*," said Dylan.

"No offense."

"Maybe you're not worse. Maybe I'm suddenly not terrible at everything," I offered. "Maybe this is finally the Year of Sam!"

Dylan did not seem comforted by the idea that it might be the Year of Sam.

"Hey, you guys," said Julie Bailey, munching a cotton candy ball the size of her head. "Everybody's racing go-karts!"

"Not me," said Dylan, slumping down between two arcade machines. "Not going to happen. I forfeit."

"What?" I said. "You love wheeled vehicles! And meaningless competitions! What's the worst that could happen?"

"I can't handle coming in last place," said Dylan. "Sorry, Sam. I think I'll just go watch the Country Gopher Family Jamboree."

"I'll find you when the race is done," I said. "Let me know if they reattached Gomer's tail!"

At the racetrack, Wilbur's party guests were busy picking out which go-karts they were going to drive. I found a sweet ride, a sleek red kart with the number twelve blazed in orange on the hood. I put on my helmet and hopped inside to pull up to the starting line.

"Oh, Sam, you can't drive number twelve," said Wilbur. "That's my go-kart."

I wanted to complain, but it was Wilbur's birthday (half a year ago).

"No problem, buddy," I said as I climbed out to pick another. "Awesome party, by the way. Thanks for the good times. Snails are cool."

By now all the good go-karts were taken.

"Hmm. There's still that one over there," said Wilbur. He pointed to a scuffed-up kart that was the color of week-old asparagus. In a slightly yellower shade of green, "#0" was painted on the back. It was, of course, the last go-kart available.

"Great," I said.

I got in and pulled number zero up to the starting line. It felt like one of the tires was smaller than the others. From beside me, Wilbur gave me a thumbs-up from behind the wheel of number twelve.

"You all know the rules or whatever," said

the racetrack attendant, another sullen teenage RaddZone employee, through a bullhorn. "Always wear your helmet. No bumping. And please, *please* keep your shoes on."

"What if they're slowing us down?" said Jared Kopernik, who had already removed one of his sneakers.

"C'mon. Do you want this whole place to smell like feet, Jared?" said the kid with the bullhorn, shaking his head. "Now, everybody on your mark. Get set . . . go or whatever."

He waved a checkered flag. The go-karts launched from the starting line. Well, most of them did. My kart puttered out onto the track at a leisurely pace as everyone else blew past. The race was three laps around a figure-eight track, and I quickly found myself at the back of the pack. So maybe it wasn't the Year of Sam after all. Maybe

CHUG! CHUG! CHUG!

Dylan really *was* just terrible.

For two laps, I bided my time and looked for an opening to (hopefully) pass somebody, anybody. My kart was sluggish and wobbly. Every time I took a curve too sharply, I heard an unhealthy rattling noise from under the hood. Still, Dylan had motivated me: I was determined not to finish last. Up ahead I saw an opening in the pack. I punched the gas as hard as I could and I felt the engine jump. Maybe old number zero had a little juice left in her after all.

Suddenly Omar Powell swerved in front of me. I pulled my foot off the gas, but somehow, the pedal stayed down. I was still accelerating. I slammed on my brakes and . . . nothing happened. The front bumper of my go-kart smacked into Omar's rear one.

"Watch it, Sam!" screamed Omar as I edged past him.

"Number zero, no bumping!" said the racetrack attendant through his bullhorn.

I hit the brakes again. Again nothing. I looked down to see that, yes, the gas pedal was permanently depressed in the "floored" position. There was something gooey underneath it. I tried to bend over and pull the pedal up, but my seat belt locked and I couldn't reach it.

KLANG! I'd let the wheel drift, and my go-kart sideswiped Drew McCoy's, causing him to spin out dangerously. Behind me I heard the squeal of other karts trying to avoid him.

"Number zero, what are you doing, man? Not cool!" yelled the racetrack attendant. "Pull over! Not cool!"

"My brakes are out!" I cried. "I can't stop accelerating and my brakes are out!"

Nobody heard me over the sound of the race. Guess that's why he had a bullhorn.

I swerved to narrowly miss Dwight Feinberg's vehicle, then Erica Spencer's. I kept on gaining speed. As I rounded the final curve, I gasped. Up ahead was the finish line. A hundred feet past it, everyone had stopped already. They were climbing out of their karts, shaking hands and congratulating one another on their final positions. They had already finished the race.

I had no way to slow down. I was going to crash right into them!

CHAPTER 5

"**E**VERYONE MOVE! GET out of the way!" I cried from my car. "I can't stop!"

But my voice was drowned out by the roar of go-kart engines and the general grand-prize/game-over racket of RaddZone. In a last-ditch effort to slow myself down, I nosed my car into the barrier that lined the track. But the rubbery wall bounced me back on course, and I was still gaining speed. I wouldn't be stopping that way. As I blew past the finish line, my position flashed on a big leaderboard: eighth place! Pretty respectable (if I wasn't about to crash in three seconds).

"Number zero, slow down!" cried the racetrack

attendant. "What are you doing? The race is over! Slow it down, bro! You're going to hurt somebody!"

A few of the finishers realized what was happening now. Somebody screamed. I hunched down in the seat and tried to imagine finishing out sixth grade in a full-body cast.

Just then I heard a mighty roar, even louder than the race. From out of nowhere an orange blur bounded over the barrier and landed twenty feet ahead, directly in my path. It was Hamstersaurus

Rex! He dug his heels in and braced for impact. I gasped, but it was too late to swerve aside. My go-kart hit him hard—but his incredible dino-strength held fast. The front bumper of number zero crumpled and the little guy slid ten feet backward, digging a pair of tiny ruts into the track. My tires squealed mightily before my vehicle finally slowed to a full stop.

"Thanks, little guy!" I cried, overcome with pride and relief.

"Hey, it's Hamstersaurus Rex!" cried Julie Bailey. "He's back!"

A cheer erupted from the other kids.

Hamstersaurus gave a strained grunt, and I realized that the back wheels of the cart were still spinning in place; the gas was still floored. I managed to untangle myself from my seat belt and bent over to get at the pedal. Sure enough, between the pedal and the floorboard was a big wad of adhesive blue goo, the sticky stuff they sell at office supply stores to put posters on walls. I yanked the pedal up and the back wheels stopped spinning. Hammie Rex exhaled. I climbed out of the go-kart and hugged him so hard he burped. The little guy had saved my life, yet again.

"My name is Una Raddenbach. I'm the owner here," said a middle-aged woman in a RaddZone striped polo shirt, who was speed-walking toward me on the track. The teen racetrack attendant trailed behind her, repeatedly brushing his floppy haircut out of his eyes.

"What happened?" said Ms. Raddenbach.

"I don't know," I said, yanking my helmet off. "The brakes on this thing don't work and it was rigged so that when I pressed the gas pedal it wouldn't come back up."

I showed her the incriminating blue sticky stuff. The other kids from the race were running toward my vehicle, too, now. They crowded around Hammie Rex and me.

"So your go-kart was . . . *sabotaged*?" said Ms. Raddenbach, looking around at Wilbur's other party guests.

"I guess?"

"Jason, check the brakes," said Ms. Raddenbach.

The shaggy-haired teen racetrack attendant,

Jason apparently, popped the hood of number zero and looked inside. He sucked air in through his teeth.

"Aw man," said Jason. "Yeah, like, the brake lines have been cut or whatever."

"Son, did you see anyone messing around with your kart?" said Ms. Raddenbach to me. "Anyone acting strangely?"

"No," I said. "I mean, nobody else wanted to drive number zero, but maybe that's just because it's painted like spoiled guacamole."

"I chose that color myself," said Ms. Raddenbach with a small frown. "Do you have enemies?"

"Yeah, lots," I said with a shrug. "But mainly they seem to be evil corporate types after my cool hamster." I held Hamstersaurus Rex up for her to see.

"He does look pretty cool," she said matter-of-factly. "All right, nobody leaves the building until we figure out exactly what happened. Jason, I want you to watch the doors. Tell R.J. and Marissa, too."

Jason nodded, flipped his hair, and ran off in the direction of the main entrance. The other

Horace Hotwater kids murmured quietly and looked askance at one another, now wondering if there was a traitor in their midst. I scanned the faces nearby, searching for the purple-haired girl in the SmilesCorp shirt I saw earlier. She was nowhere to be seen.

"Now," said Ms. Raddenbach, eyeing the other kids, "which one of you—"

Suddenly there was a loud pop and RaddZone went dark. A hush fell over the place. The only light was the faint red glow of the emergency exits scattered around the cavernous space.

"What in the name of . . . ?" cried Ms. Raddenbach, storming off. "What's going on? Turn the lights back on! R.J.! Marissa!"

"It's a power outage!" one of the kids screamed.

"It's aliens!" someone else screamed.

"Don't be ridiculous," screamed a third person. "It's the ghost of Horace Hotwater!"

And after that it was pure panic.

CHAPTER 6

KIDS WERE RUNNING around in the darkness, shrieking in mindless terror. Omar Powell crawled under his go-kart. Tina Gomez yanked at her hair and fled toward the ball pits, howling about a supernatural evil that she "foresaw in a dream." Two of my frightened classmates smacked into each other at full speed and fell to the floor. It might have been Jimmy Choi and Caroline Moody, but it was too dark to tell for sure.

"Guys, it's not the ghost of Horace Hotwater!" I yelled to no one in particular. "If he haunts our middle school—which he doesn't—then he can't haunt here, too. Ghosts only haunt one place. That's how ghosts work. And also they're not real!"

My argument was confusing, even to me. And the nuances were clearly lost on the panicking mob of sixth graders. It suddenly occurred to me that whoever had messed with my go-kart was still right here, lurking somewhere in the dark, with me. I shuddered.

"Hammie, is Cartimandua safe?" I said.

He hopped up and down and gave a little yip. He wasn't worried about her.

"Cool. Then we need to find Dylan!"

The little guy snarled with what might have been cold resolve (or indigestion) and we set out across RaddZone.

I navigated my way through the labyrinth of depowered arcade games on the ground level. The Country Gopher Family Jamboree was in a small amphitheater with a curtained stage in the center; the name was proudly displayed on a sign styled to look like a network of gopher tunnels. The outage had apparently happened in the middle of the show. The animatronic Country Gophers were all frozen midperformance, their rubbery faces contorted into grotesque smiles as they clutched their banjos and washboards. Hammie Rex snarled at them. I felt the same way. In the dark, right after someone had tried to engineer your fiery go-kart demise, the Country Gopher Family Jamboree didn't look so funny after all.

"Dylan?" I called out. My voice echoed through the empty amphitheater. No one called back. "You here?"

I headed back out onto the main arcade floor. "Hey, Dylan!" I yelled louder. Still no answer. Had something happened to Dylan?

"Sam, look out!"

Dylan tackled me off my feet and onto the floor. Hammie Rex yelped in surprise as he tumbled out of my shirt pocket.

"Easy, Dylan," I said. "Look, are you still mad I beat you at air hockey? Because, honestly, I don't know how I did—"

KRASH! Right where I had been standing, a massive object hit the floor and exploded into bits! I covered my face as I was showered with splinters of wood and circuit board. It took me a second to realize that the thing that had almost flattened me was an old-school arcade game. It took me another second to see that it was a vintage copy of Ms. Super Plunger Jr.

"So they *did* have it," I said, shaking my head in disbelief.

"I saw it fall from up there," said Dylan, pointing. "Look!"

A shadowy figure stood by the railing of the second level. An instant later, the person was gone. Hammie Rex roared.

"That Ms. Super Plunger Jr. cabinet *had* to weigh three hundred pounds," I said. "How could somebody just fling it over the railing like that?"

"No idea," cried Dylan. "I'd kill for core strength like that. Imagine how far I could throw a golf disc. Anyway, we can discuss their workout regimen after we catch them!" She was on her feet and running for the stairs. Hammie Rex was right behind her.

"Hang on!" I cried, following as quickly as I could. "Wait for me!"

Owing to her years of relentless sports training, Dylan was the fastest of the three of us. She made it up to the second level well ahead of Hamstersaurus Rex, who had substantially shorter legs. I pulled up the rear, huffing and puffing like the (let's face it) indoor kid I was. Sixty feet away stood the shadowy figure we'd seen before. I could now

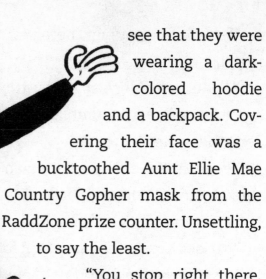

see that they were wearing a dark-colored hoodie and a backpack. Covering their face was a bucktoothed Aunt Ellie Mae Country Gopher mask from the RaddZone prize counter. Unsettling, to say the least.

"You stop right there, you!" I cried.

Aunt Ellie Mae ducked behind a row of pinball machines and disappeared. Dylan took off again.

"Oh, you can run, Aunt Ellie Mae," cried Dylan as she charged, "but you can't—"

Dylan's feet shot out from under her, and she hit the ground face-first and skidded into one of those penny-flattening machines with a sickening thud.

"Whoa, are you okay?" I caught up to where she lay and crouched down beside her. Hammie Rex gently licked her knuckles.

Dylan winced and clutched at her leg. "Ow. I think I slipped on something . . ." She trailed off and pointed to the floor behind her. Next to a trash can full of RaddSpudds, a carelessly discarded sour cream packet oozed its contents all over the floor. I saw a telltale smear where Dylan's foot had hit it and skidded.

"A sour cream slick," I said. "Can you still run?"

"Yeah, I'm pretty sure I can," said Dylan, trying to get up. "Just need to . . . argh!" She grunted and slumped back down to the ground, grabbing at her ankle. I could see that her right ankle was already swelling up like a water balloon.

"I think it might be sprained," I said.

"It's the curse," said Dylan.

"It's *not* the curse," I said. "Just bad luck. Maybe we should wrap it so it doesn't—"

"Don't worry about me, Sam. Aunt Ellie Mae is getting away," said Dylan.

I nodded and leaped to my feet. Hammie and I ran after the hooded figure. As we rounded the row of pinball machines, I saw that we were at the entrance to Mount Putta-Putta, the complex's mini-golf course. Aunt Ellie Mae had retreated inside.

The course was nine holes, winding its way up the cone of the fake volcano that, three times a day, erupted with a blast of dry ice and confetti. I knew from playing the Mount Putta-Putta that there was one way in and one way out, through the entrance gate we'd just passed.

"Ha. Now we've got 'em," I whispered to Hamstersaurus Rex as I grabbed a blue putter off the rack. "She might not know it, but Aunt Ellie Mae is trapped in here."

Hammie and I carefully began to make our ascent. At the third hole, the little guy froze.

"What is it, boy?" I hissed. "What's wrong?"

Before he could respond, a massive wooden tiki god came bouncing, end over end, down the slope toward us. Hammie and I dove out of the way, and it took out a straw hut behind us. Up ahead, Aunt Ellie Mae disappeared around the cone.

"Come on!" I cried.

Hamstersaurus Rex gave a mighty roar and

we ran after the gopher-faced figure. At the seventh hole, we were nearly crushed again, this time under a gigantic plaster sea turtle. If I hadn't stopped to tie my shoe an instant earlier, I would have been a goner for sure. The turtle had been flung from even higher up on the course: specifically, the ninth hole, the very crater of Mount Putta-Putta.

As we crested the top of the fake volcano, it suddenly occurred to me that I might actually *catch* the person under that gopher mask. What was I going to do then? The little blue putter in my hand suddenly seemed inadequate.

"Careful, Hammie," I said. "Whoever that is, they're crazy strong. That sea turtle probably weighed as much as a refrigerator."

Hammie and I crept around the corner, approaching the ninth hole. The crater of Mount Putta-Putta was painted in bright reds and oranges to simulate the lava flow of an active volcano. Fake paper flames now hung limp beside the fans that normally made them flicker and dance. If you were playing Mount Putta-Putta, when you made your final putt, your ball rolled down a tube all the way back down to a big basket behind the front desk. If you got a hole in one—which I did once in second grade; maybe *that* was the Year of Sam?—RaddZone gave you a free RaddSpudd.

I certainly wished I were eating a RaddSpudd at that moment, instead of facing off against a masked psycho who was buff enough to toss around wooden tiki gods.

Hamstersaurus Rex stopped in his tracks. Up ahead, I saw the shadowy figure standing perfectly still; their back was to us, hood up.

"Freeze," I said, my voice wavering. "You're, uh, under arrest . . . I guess?" I could see the putter in my hands shaking. Beside me, Hamstersaurus Rex bellowed. He sounded a lot more confident.

"Hmm," said the figure in an eerie high-pitched voice, like the sound of metal scraping on metal. "We think not."

I had a strange feeling on my skin, like when you rub a balloon on your arm and the static collects. Then from out of nowhere, a surfboard came whistling through the air, its point aimed right at my head. Before I could react, Hamster-saurus Rex sprang and somehow caught it in his dinosaur jaws mid-flight. His sideways momen-tum deflected the board's deadly trajectory, so that it missed me by a couple of feet. Instead of skewering my head, it smashed to pieces against the inside rim of the volcano.

The masked figure had turned to face us now. The mouth of the Aunt Ellie Mae mask was a ghoulish bucktoothed grin; the eyeholes were two pools of shadow.

"Bravo," came that irritating squeak-voice. "Another so-called act of 'heroism.' I suppose you think you're so special because everyone adores you, while they all despise us? Well, when we're through with you, we think you'll find that you're *not so special after all!*"

With a growl, Hamstersaurus Rex launched himself at the masked figure. The little guy chomped on to Aunt Ellie Mae's calf, which elic-ited a loud squeal of pain. Aunt Ellie Mae tripped and stumbled over backward, causing her back-pack to go flying. The pack bounced across the ground and came to rest near my feet with the flap open. I moved toward it and then stopped. Was I crazy, or had the bag twitched? It twitched again. I wasn't crazy. Something inside the back-pack was alive.

I crouched to peer into the pack's opening. For an instant, the faint light caught two beady eyes inside, gleaming yellow. There was something about those eyes . . . something . . .

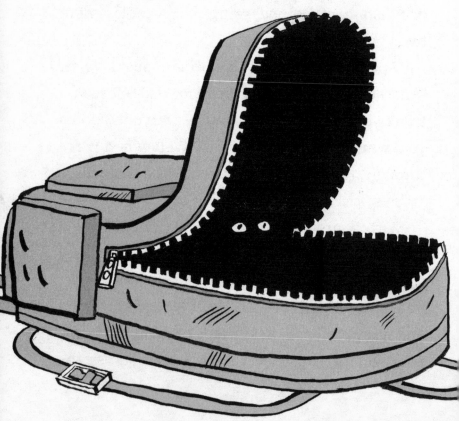

"Sam?" It was Dylan's voice farther down Mount Putta-Putta. "Don't worry! I'm coming!"

I blinked. With a piercing squeal, a small, furry creature shot out of the pack and disappeared into the ninth hole. I dove for the hole, but I was too late. Whatever the thing was, it was already out of reach, down into the endless pipe.

I turned to see that Hammie Rex still had his dino-jaws locked in a death grip on Aunt Ellie Mae's pant leg. Aunt Ellie Mae struggled and fought, but she was no match for the prehistoric might of Hamstersaurus Rex.

"Time to find out who you really are," I said, and I yanked off the Country Gopher mask.

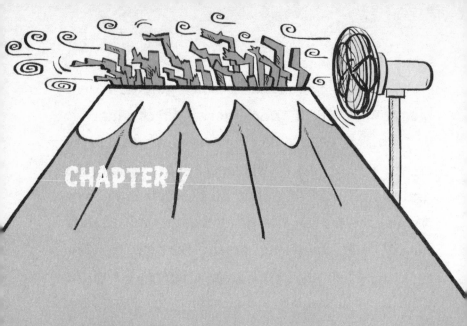

CHAPTER 7

"**W**ILBUR WEBER?!" I cried.

In the darkness, Wilbur's face was twisted into an imperious sneer. From above, there came a loud crackle. And then the lights of RaddZone flickered on. All around me I heard the bells and buzzers and other sounds of countless video games coming back to life. The fans started blowing and the fake flames of Mount Putta-Putta began to dance once more. Wilbur blinked in the bright light.

"Whoa. Am I at . . . RaddZone?" he said slowly as he took in his surroundings. "Suh-weeeeet."

"What? Of *course* you're at RaddZone," I said,

76

grabbing him by the hoodie and yanking him to his feet. "You tried to kill me for your birthday!"

"Um. My birthday was in June," said Wilbur.

"Why?" I yelled. "Why did you sabotage my go-kart? Why did you try to drop Ms. Super Plunger Jr. on me? What have you got against me, Wilbur?"

"Nothing," said Wilbur, "I don't know what you're talking about, Sam. But maybe I should get going. I think I'm late for—"

"Stay right there!" I yelled.

Wilbur took a tentative step, but Hamstersaurus Rex gave him a Cretaceous death stare that froze him in place.

I reached in Wilbur's backpack and found exactly what I expected. "If you didn't cut my brakes or mess with my gas pedal," I said, "then explain these." I held up a pair of wire cutters and several empty packages of the sticky blue office goo.

"Those aren't mine," said Wilbur slowly.

"You're not getting off the hook by playing dumb, Wilbur," I said. "You tried to crush me with a sea turtle!"

"Listen to yourself," said Wilbur. "You sound nuts."

"Only I'm guessing it wasn't you who was so strong after all, was it?" I said. "It was that nasty little critter in your backpack. I get it now. It's another Squirrel Kong situation. You've got some crazy vendetta, so you're using a freaky mutant animal with superstrength to attack me and Hamstersaurus Rex!"

"I'm not doing that," said Wilbur.

"So what is it? Some kind of ferret on steroids? A chipmunk that was bitten by a radioactive gorilla? *What?*"

"You're scaring me, Sam."

"Quit faking!" I roared. Wilbur whimpered and shrank away from me.

"Sam!"

I heard Dylan behind me. She'd somehow hobbled all the way up the course using a golf club as a makeshift crutch.

"You caught him," said Dylan. "No need to lose your cool."

"I know, I know," I said, "but he's pretending like he didn't do anything!"

"Let him pretend," said Dylan. "It won't change the truth. I saw him, too."

Dylan, Hamstersaurus Rex, and I slowly escorted Wilbur back down Mount Putta-Putta. Wilbur protested his innocence the whole time. Dylan winced with each step. At the front desk of the course, I checked the ball basket to see if there were any evil rodents. There weren't. The beast was long gone. Of course, Wilbur wouldn't say *where* it had gone.

Una Raddenbach was waiting for us on the ground level, flanked by her teen employees and all of Wilbur's party guests, who stood in stunned silence. Jimmy Choi and Caroline Moody each had a black eye. The purple-haired girl was nowhere to be seen.

"Here he is," I said. "The kid who destroyed a vintage arcade game and a fake sea turtle and sabotaged my go-kart in the name of evil."

"Plus he stole an Aunt Ellie Mae Gopher mask from the prize counter," added Dylan. "That thing's worth over three thousand tickets."

"You're in a world of trouble, son," said Ms. Raddenbach, taking Wilbur by the elbow and pulling him toward her office. "We're calling your parents. Possibly the police."

"But I didn't do any of that stuff," said Wilbur quietly. Then he sniffled, and a second later he was bawling his eyes out. "I m-m-m-miss my sn-sn-sn-snaaaaaails!" he wailed. It was a disgusting display.

"Don't believe the tears," I said. "Wilbur Weber is an evil genius."

"Well, evil, anyway," said Dylan.

"I'm sorry I ever wished him happy birthday,"

said Tina Gomez, removing her party hat like it was radioactive.

"This whole thing seems like more of a Beefer Vanderkoff move than a Wilbur Weber endeavor," said Julie Bailey.

"Go-kart sabotage; power outage, falling arcade games," said Jimmy Choi, rubbing his shiner. "Worst party ever."

"The RaddSpudds were good, though," said Jared Kopernik, biting into one.

"Seriously," said Caroline Moody, "it's only thanks to Hamstersaurus Rex that nobody was killed!"

There was a murmur of approval for Hamstersaurus Rex. He looked bashful in my palm.

Ms. Raddenbach paused. "Um, totally unrelated question, kids," she said. "None of your parents are, um, lawyers, are they?"

"My mom is," said Omar Powell.

"Both mine are," said Lucy Khan.

"Mine, too," said Drew McKoy.

"You know what?" said Ms. Raddenbach. "Free RaddSpudds for life for all of you . . ."

"Yay!" the kids screamed.

". . . if you sign a waiver saying that neither RaddZone nor I are legally liable for anything that may or may not have happened today!" continued Ms. Raddenbach.

"Yay?" screamed the kids, a bit more tentatively.

After signing a nine-page contract with a two-page nondisclosure rider, we each got a RaddSpudd in a red foil wrapper with a picture of Gomer Gopher on it. Hammie Rex ate mine. He earned it. Apparently we could get another one for free any time we came back ("no hole-in-one required; limit one per patron per visit"). The only hitch was that RaddZone would remain closed for the foreseeable future. Ms. Raddenbach assured us it was totally unrelated to the series of near-fatal incidents that may or may not have occurred at Wilbur's party. Really, she just wanted to spend a bit more time with her family.

As for families, all of us sixth graders called our parents and waited. Through the window to Ms. Raddenbach's office I could see Wilbur Weber sobbing quietly as he waited for his mom and dad to come pick him up. I didn't get it. Aside from an unflattering caricature long ago, what had I ever done to him? Even he seemed to be confused about why he was out to get me. Was it possible he was simply a SmilesCorp pawn? Had he gotten into something over his head? It just didn't make sense.

"Well, evil has been thwarted," said Dylan. "Even if I'm still cursed." After the adrenaline of the chase wore off, Dylan could barely walk on her sprained ankle. It had turned a kind of sickly purplish color.

"Sorry about your ankle," I said. "But you're not cursed. And evil hasn't been thwarted. What about the nasty little varmint that Wilbur had in his backpack? It can toss around three-hundred-pound arcade machines like they're nothing. What if it's the real danger, not Wilbur?"

"You're right. We have to stop it!" said Dylan, rising heroically and then clenching her jaw in pain and flopping back down.

"I think you should probably go see a doctor first," I said, scratching underneath

Hamstersaurus Rex's furry jaw.

"You're probably right about that, too," said Dylan. "Hey, didn't you come here with two hamsters?"

"Oh yeah!" Somehow I had totally forgotten Cartimandua. I raced back to the Love Tester machine. Luckily she was still asleep, exactly where I'd left her. She blinked as I scooped her up.

"You know, Cartimandua, Hamstersaurus Rex proved he was a big hero today," I said.

Hamstersaurus Rex puffed out his little chest. Cartimandua yawned and went to sleep again. Hammie wilted. I tucked them both in my pockets and headed for the doors.

Outside, a line of sensible parental vehicles lined the curb in front of RaddZone. I helped Dylan to her dad's SUV. He was concerned about her ankle, but Dylan tried to play it off as no big deal. I think she was embarrassed about being taken out by a baked potato topping. After that, I climbed into my mom's car.

"Hi, Bunnybutt," she said. "How was the big party at RaddZone?"

"I beat Dylan at air hockey," I said.

"Not bad!"

"And Wilbur Weber wants to kill me."

"The snails kid?"

"The snails kid."

"Well, that's just—ACHOOOOOOOO!" My mom let out a sneeze so powerful it put Mount Putta-Putta's eruption to shame. She's highly allergic to anything with fur, and I had not one but two hamsters in my pocket.

"Oh, and I got, uh, covered in some pet hair," I lied. "Sorry."

My mom's eyes were already tearing up. Her nose was erupting like Mount Putta-Putta. "Pet hair?" she sniffled. "At RaddZone?"

"Yeah. Wilbur had a weird little animal with him. I think it's pretty dangerous. Maybe, like, a ferret on steroids. I think I need to report it."

"Tonight?"

"Tonight."

Later that evening, after I'd safely dropped Hamstersaurus Rex and Cartimandua off at home, my mom and I pulled into Maple Bluffs Animal Control to find that the parking lot was totally full. My mom decided to wait in the car, wiping her runny nose, for fear of encountering even more pet hair if she went in.

It felt a little weird walking toward the front door. Not too long ago, animal control agents were hunting for Hamstersaurus Rex. Still, it was my best option for professional help.

Inside was a cluttered and dingy office that smelled a bit like wet dog. The place was absolutely packed. Maple Bluffs citizens crowded around the front desk. Behind it sat the town's two animal control agents, Anne Gould and Ralph McKay, looking utterly overwhelmed. This didn't look like their typical weekday evening workload.

". . . I saw it swimming in my swimming pool," said Mr. Haddad, who owned a paint-it-yourself pottery shop in town. "And that was when I realized that it didn't have feathers at all. *It had fur.*"

"And you're sure it wasn't a platypus?" said McKay.

"No, it wasn't a platypus! Don't be ridiculous,"

said Mr. Haddad. "It was a duck with fur!"

I felt a jolt of recognition. I'd seen a duck with fur before, inside the SmilesCorp animal lab. I'd broken into the place with Beefer on a dual mission to figure out how to stop Squirrel Kong and rescue Beefer's missing snake, Michael Perkins. Then Squirrel Kong had burst in through a wall and, well, things had gotten a little out of hand.

"Furry duck? That's nothing," said Ms. Maxwell, the former librarian. "I was in the park doing my yogas and I saw a dachshund with six legs. It was frolicking around without a care in the world, *like it had the correct number of legs*! I practically died."

"Dachshund. Six legs," said Gould, writing as fast as she could.

"I saw a chicken that looked exactly like a turtle!" yelled Craig Lindley, a gas station attendant.

"Maybe it *was* a turtle," said McKay.

"Don't patronize me!" said Craig Lindley.

"My toolshed is full of scaly white mice!" said Milos Schweyer, who owned a construction company. He shuddered. "I'm scared to go in there."

Old Man Ohlman elbowed his way to the

front of the crowd. He was Maple Bluffs's resident crackpot—never without his shiny tinfoil hat—who could often be seen on Main Street, arguing with manhole covers and occasionally apologizing to them.

"The other day I stepped outside and there was a mole and it looked at me real mean!" cried Old Man Ohlman. "No man should suffer to be looked at like that by a mole. T'ain't right, I tell ya. T'ain't right!"

"Mean mole," said Gould. "Okay. Got it."

"Nobody cares about the turtle chicken?" cried Craig Lindley. "Seriously?!"

It seemed that weirdo animals were everywhere! And I knew exactly where they came from. They were all SmilesCorp escapees, inadvertently set free when Squirrel Kong attacked. They sounded strange, sure. But from what I could tell, none of them were trying to hurt people, unlike the horrible little beast in Wilbur's backpack.

I eventually nudged my way to the front desk and waited for a break in the complaining to make my own complaint.

"Um, hi," I said. "My name is Sam Gibbs. We've met before."

Agent Gould cocked her head. "Did we remove a live trout from your toilet tank?"

"No, no," I said. "There was a thing with a squirrel. Anyway, I'd like to report another strange animal in town."

She sighed. "Great. Go ahead."

"Well, it was small and furry and superstrong," I said.

"What kind of animal was it?"

"Not sure. It could have been a rat. Or maybe a mongoose? But you should be careful. It's really dangerous."

"Anything else?"

"It had these little . . . eyes. They were intense."

"Little furry animal, superstrong," she narrated as she wrote. "Penetrating gaze."

"So you think you'll be able to catch it?" I said.

"As you can see, we're swamped right now. I'll add your complaint to the end of the queue," said Gould. "Looks like it's"—she flipped through her notepad—"number fifty-three. We'll investigate when we have time. Maybe next month? That's the best we can do."

"But that thing is still out there," I said. "It could hurt someone."

"Sorry, kid," said Gould. "I've got a furry duck and a bunch of scaly mice to bring to justice first."

I walked back outside toward my mom's

car. It was night now. The streetlights of Maple Bluffs twinkled in the darkness. A cool breeze made me shiver. Once again, a horrible mutant creature was on the loose, and once again it was up to me and Hamstersaurus Rex to stop it.

CHAPTER 8

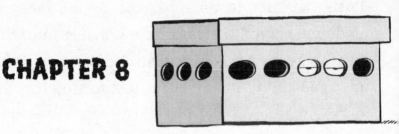

THAT NIGHT, I periodically checked on Cartimandua in her shoebox in the garage. From what I could tell she stayed awake the whole time, apparently fascinated by the prospect of several completely new walls to stare at. Hamstersaurus Rex stayed awake in his hypoallergenic habitat, too. I think that with Cartimandua there, he was just too nervous to sleep.

The next morning I got to school early and quickly dropped off Hammie at Meeting Club HQ. Then I went to sneak Cartimandua back into her cage before anyone noticed she was missing.

The hallway was clear, so I ducked inside Mr.

Copeland's classroom and unlocked the PETCA-TRAZ Pro™.

"Hello, Sam." Martha slowly swiveled in Mr. Copeland's chair to face me. She did not look happy.

"Whoa," I said, jumping roughly three feet in the air while simultaneously trying to hide Cartimandua behind my back. "Hiya, Martha! How's it going?"

"Not well," she said, steepling her fingers. "Not well at all."

"Oh, what seems to be the problem? Did you get an A-minus or something? Crazy weather we've been having lately. Lots of clouds. Too many? How's the Antique Doll Museum? I like drawing. Talk to you soon. Gotta go. Bye." I started to back toward the door.

"Not so fast," said Martha. "Where's Cartimandua?"

I looked at the empty hamster cage. I looked at Martha. I looked back at the empty hamster cage. "Oh no!" I said. "She's been kidnapped!"

"It was a rhetorical question," said Martha.

"You're holding her behind your back right now."

"Um, case closed," I said, gently placing Cartimandua back in her cage and patting her on the head. "This was, uh, a test. And you passed, Martha. You're a fantastic Hamster Monitor. And also very intelligent in general. Has anyone ever told you that?"

"Most authority figures and all standardized tests," said Martha, crossing her arms. "Sam, what did I say about taking Cartimandua out of her cage?"

I sighed. "Not to do it."

"So why did you disobey a direct order from your Hamster Monitor commanding officer?"

"*Commanding officer?* As I recall, you quit and promoted me and—and it's just lanyards you printed and cut out at home anyway! Look, I was just trying to spread a little love in this cruel world. Two lonely hamsters finding a connection! So I took Cartimandua to RaddZone. What's the big deal?"

"The big deal? I heard that Wilbur's party was rife with go-kart sabotage and falling tiki gods!

Cartimandua could have been killed!"

She was right, of course. And that annoyed me even more.

"Oh, I'm just fine, thanks for asking," I said. "None of that stuff was about her, you know. Not sure if Wilbur Weber lost his mind or he's working for SmilesCorp or what, but he had some sort of . . . *creature*, and it attacked Hamstersaurus Rex and me! Cartimandua snoozed through the whole thing."

"Like it or not, Hamstersaurus Rex is a target," said Martha. "First Beefer was out to get him. Then Squirrel Kong and Roberta Fast. Now it's Wilbur's deranged animal familiar. Wherever Hamstersaurus Rex is, danger follows."

"That's not his fault," I said. "Just because he's got awesome dino-powers, it seems like every creep and crazy in the world wants to take him out."

"Exactly! That puts those around Hamstersaurus Rex—you, me, Dylan—at risk," said Martha. "It's bad enough that you somehow convinced me to hide him in that closet instead of in a PETCA-TRAZ Pro™ under twenty-four-hour surveillance.

I may not be able to protect him, but I can at least make sure nothing bad happens to Cartimandua."

"Nothing will!"

"From this moment on, Cartimandua will not leave her cage, except under my direct supervision. Do you understand?" said Martha. "And for the indefinite future, I'm putting you on Hamster Monitor desk duty."

"No fair!" I said, and stormed out. I was halfway down the hall before I realized I didn't even understand what Hamster Monitor desk duty was.

I swung by Meeting Club HQ again to check in on Hamstersaurus Rex. The little guy was lying facedown, emitting a soft, continuous moan. I had a feeling this was Cartimandua-related. After all, RaddZone hadn't been a very successful hamster date. If only I could help him feel better somehow. But the ways of the hamster heart were still a mystery to me. Poor Hammie Rex.

"Cheer up, pal," I said. "Remember when you saved me from that deadly surfboard attack? Your old buddy Sam: not dead, because of you. Yay."

He kept on moaning. I turned off the light and

quietly closed the door.

I waited by the sixth-grade lockers for the first bell to ring. Wilbur didn't show up to school. But Dylan did, on crutches. On her foot was a cast and one of those bulky medical boots.

"So how bad is the sprain?" I said.

"Luckily no sprain," she said. "It's the hairline fracture of the tibia that's the problem. I broke my ankle, Sam. On sour cream."

"I knew that stuff was bad for you," I offered weakly. "Er, sorry, Dylan."

Dylan sighed. "I'll probably be on the disabled list for the rest of the disc golf season. Also I flunked yesterday's history quiz. Oh, and on the way to school, two birds pooped on my head."

"Two birds?"

"Separate incidents," said Dylan ominously. "Don't stand too close to me, Sam. Unless you want to get struck by lightning."

"It's just bad luck."

"This goes beyond bad luck," said Dylan. "It's the curse of Horace Hotwater's ghost!"

"Horace Hotwater's ghost?" said Tina Gomez,

overhearing us. "Maybe that's who took my irre-placeable pencil eraser."

"I *saw* you replace it!" I said.

"If I had my camera, maybe I could take a picture of the ghost," said Dwight Feinberg. "But I don't. Because nobody solved the Case of Dwight Feinberg's Missing Camera." He gave a heavy sigh.

"I'll find your camera, Dwight," I said.

"I wouldn't hold out too much hope," said Jared Kopernik. "The ghost probably ate it."

"Ghosts don't eat," I said. "How is it that I don't even believe in ghosts and yet I seem to be the only one at this school who knows *anything* about them?!"

The other kids shrugged.

"Look, I'll admit some strange things have been going down around here lately. But I'm sure there's a reasonable explanation," I said. "Prob-ably related to weird animals of some kind."

"Speaking of weird animals, where's Hamster-saurus Rex?" said Julie Bailey. "I thought today would mark his triumphant return to school and

I wanted to present him with this tiny homemade medal of valor." She held up a lentil with thread glued to it.

"He's, well, he's just kind of lying low for a while," I said. I dropped my voice to a whisper. "Because he's on a very important detective stealth mission." I tapped the side of my nose.

"So cool," said Julie. "I'll make him another medal for espionage!"

The bell rang. Dylan and I continued on to our classroom.

"Don't worry," I said. "I'm going to put this whole ghost thing to rest today."

"You're going to investigate the haunted basement?" said Dylan.

"Yup, Hammie and I will check it out," I said. "I bet Wilbur's beast somehow did the flying bulletin board trick with its . . . superstrength. Anyway, you're welcome to come along if you want."

"I, uh, totally would," said Dylan, tensing up, "but, you know, my ankle and stuff . . ." She trailed off and stared at the floor.

"Right," I said. "No worries." I didn't press it,

but I could tell she was terrified. I wasn't used to seeing her like this. Normally she wasn't afraid of anything.

"Just be careful," said Dylan.

"Don't worry about me," I said. "I know Horace Hotwater's weakness."

"You do?"

"Yep. Chunky soup."

Dylan didn't laugh.

The school day passed without incident. Did I learn anything? I'd like to think that I did. We don't need to get into specifics. Anyway, after the final bell rang, I made my way to Meeting Club HQ. I found Hammie Rex lying facedown, right where I'd left him.

"All right, pal, up and at 'em!" I said. "You're the hamster champion of all that is good and right in this nutty world. Time to confront the mysterious evil that may or may not lurk in our school's spooky basement!"

The little guy didn't move. Today, he was the hamster champion of moping.

"I know you're still bummed out," I said. "But

you know what that poster at the dentist's office says: 'A frown is just a smile that needs to get flipped sunny-side up! Always remember to floss!' Hmm. Now that I'm saying it out loud, I feel like the first part is more relevant. Anyway, time to go."

With a pitiful sigh, Hamstersaurus Rex rolled over onto his back and stared up at nothing in particular. I practically had to scrape the little guy off the floor.

"We have to be prepared for whatever we find at the bottom of those stairs," I said as I carried him down the deserted hallway. "I'm ninety-nine percent sure it's not a pioneer ghost, but it's sure to be something weird, possibly a ferret on steroids. Maybe a bionic lemming? High alert, okay?"

Hamstersaurus Rex squinted at me and made a noise that was almost like "ugh." He'd certainly never done that before.

I paused at the top of the creepy basement stairs. Once again I got that strange staticky feeling, like the hairs on my neck were standing up. I felt my no-ghost confidence dropping a few percentage points. I wanted to turn around and go home. Instead I took a deep breath and headed down.

Inside the stairwell, the cinder-block walls were scrawled with graffiti that, in my imagination, took on a sinister tone. "Fuzz Was Here." *Okay, so where was Fuzz now? What happened to Fuzz? Why won't anyone tell me what happened to Fuzz?!*

At the bottom of the stairs there was on old wooden chair with a broken leg—perhaps set aside to be repaired by a custodian, but long ago forgotten. Behind it was a rusty door that said "Boiler Room." Through that door, I could hear the heave and groan of Horace Hotwater's heating system. At least, I hoped that's what was groaning.

"You ready, pal?" I whispered to Hammie.

He looked at me with forlorn, red-rimmed eyes and whined. I paused.

"You know what? You're right. I'm way too scared to go through that spooky door, too," I said. "We should probably just turn around and leave.

On account of being total chickens."

I turned very slowly, as though I meant to walk back up the stairs.

Hamstersaurus Rex growled. Then he shook himself like a dog that had run through a sprinkler. The little guy pawed the door, and I could now see that a bit of his old vim and vigor had returned. The reverse psychology had worked.

"Now that's more like it," I said.

I pushed the door, and it swung inward with a tortured creak. . . .

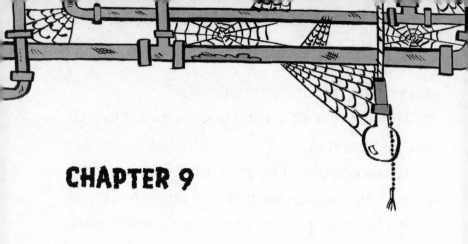

CHAPTER 9

BEHIND THAT CREEPY door was . . . a boiler room. There were no ominous pools of blood. No werewolves. No masked, machete-wielding lurkers. Not even a stray cat to knock something over and give us a false scare. Instead there was just a hot-water heater, some rusty pipes, and lots and lots of cobwebs. A single dangling bulb lit the small room. With the light on, it wasn't even that creepy. I almost felt disappointed. Still, I had to make a full investigation. I owed Dylan that much.

I turned the light off again and pulled out my UltraLite SmartShot digital camera. Then I set it to night-vision mode. Not sure why, but night-vision mode is what all the "paranormal investigators" on TV use when they're looking for ghosts.

"Um, hello. Hi . . . I mean, er, greetings," I stammered into the camera. I usually worked with a script. "Are there any, you know, ghosts here?"

No answer. I panned the camera left and right and watched the swimming green shapes on the LCD screen. I saw a fuzzy white shape. Was that a ghost? No, it was my thumb on the lens.

"Specifically," I continued, "is the ghost of Horace Hotwater—the shorts-wearing founder of Maple Bluffs who died in a tragic soup-related accident—here in this room?"

No answer.

"If there are any ghosts, spirits, demons, or Frankensteins, please give me a sign."

From the corner, Hamstersaurus Rex made a whining noise. I hadn't been watching him, but the little guy was sniffing and scratching at the baseboard. I turned the lights back on and walked toward him.

"What are you looking at, pal?" I said.

Hammie Rex whined again and stomped his

foot. I noticed that the floor around him was considerably less dusty than the rest of the room. I bent down to inspect the baseboard.

"Looks normal," I said.

Hammie Rex growled and banged his head against the baseboard. When he did, I could hear a hollow ring. I slowly traced my fingers along the baseboard. Sure enough, I felt a seam. I pulled on it, and a section came loose. Behind it was a dark, circular tunnel, about six inches wide, right into the foundation of the building. I crouched and looked in. I couldn't see very far, but I could tell that it went all the way through the concrete, into the dirt beyond.

"Okay, that's a little creepy," I said. "Probably shouldn't do this, but here goes." I took a deep breath and plunged my hand into the hole. Luckily nothing bit me. My arm went in as far as my shoulder but didn't reach the end.

"Hmm. I think this might be a job for you, pal," I said to Hamstersaurus Rex.

I had an idea. Using a rubber band, I carefully mounted my UltraLite SmartShot onto Hamstersaurus Rex's head. Then I wirelessly synced it with the old laptop that I used for editing my films (such unreleased future blockbusters as *Chinchillazilla vs. MechaChinchillazilla* and *Abraham Lincoln Was a Hamster?!*). I fiddled with the inputs, and suddenly I could see what Hammie Rex was seeing, live, in real time.

"All right," I said. "Time to spelunk."

Hamstersaurus Rex grunted and trotted into the tunnel. I watched on my laptop. It kind of looked like a first-person-shooter video game, all in monochrome green. I could see that the tunnel ran for about three feet and then opened onto a wider chamber.

"Whoa," I said as Hammie looked from right to left, swiveling the camera with the turning of his head.

The chamber was filled with a weird assortment of debris. Shredded junk food wrappers carpeted the floor. Something glinted among them. It was a shiny, rumpled cloth. I could just make out A-M-A-T-O in block letters.

"Wait a second," I said. "That's Dylan's away jersey!"

By one wall, I saw a chemical canister that appeared to have come from the school lab. I noticed a pop-up book from the library called *Dinosaurs Are Neat!* There was also a self-help book for grown-ups called *How to Not Be Unlikable*. Beside it was a comic book, *The Legend of Max Stomper #338*, with several pages torn out.

"And that's the comic book that Drew McCoy is missing!"

Near the books was a gnawed pencil nub and a worn-down eraser.

"And that's Tina Gomez's eraser!" I said.

As Hammie Rex continued to turn his head, I gasped. An

instant camera—the kind that spits out photos right after you take them—lay in the dirt. It had to be Dwight Feinberg's!

Rex & Gibbs had just closed three cases in one fell swoop. But that wasn't the most shocking thing about the weird little cache of items. The final wall was covered with surveillance photos of Hamstersaurus Rex! They were taken at a distance and in various locations, sometimes with me and sometimes without. It was clear that Hammie hadn't been aware of the photographer. I know I wasn't. Mixed in with the snapshots were clippings from our local newspaper, the *Maple Bluffs Bee-Intelligencer*: there was an article about the Science Night when Hamstersaurus Rex fought Michael Perkins. There was another about Principal Truitt offering Hamstersaurus Rex a novelty check to thank him for his heroics at the disc golf tournament. The place was like a spooky shrine to the little guy.

"What the heck?" I said under my breath.

Just then, I heard someone coming down the basement stairs.

CHAPTER 10

"**H**AMMIE, THE CROISSANT is out of the oven," I whispered. "Repeat: the croissant is out of the oven!"

When we'd started being detectives, we'd worked out a bunch of secret codes. Either the little guy didn't hear me, or he'd forgotten what "the croissant is out of the oven" was code for. Come to think of it, maybe I'd forgotten what it was code for. It was either "Somebody's coming" or "Destroy the dossier." I wrote it down somewhere. But where?

Agh! Whoever it was, was nearly at the bottom of the steps now. As much as I didn't like the thought of trapping Hammie inside the hole, we were out of time. I hastily replaced the loose section of the baseboard and leaped to my feet. Then I turned the light off and frantically looked around for a hiding spot. There were no good ones, so I dove behind the boiler itself, careful not to touch it and burn myself. I crouched there in the dust as still as I could, trying not to think about spiders. Now I could see a shadow in the slice of light beneath the door.

The door slowly creaked open. Silhouetted in the door frame was an odd man wearing an obviously fake, white beard and a ludicrously oversized ten-gallon hat. Despite the "disguise," it took me approximately four milliseconds to recognize him: it was none other than Gordon Renfro, Horace Hotwater Middle School's recently departed science teacher, who had gone by the alias "Todd Duderotti" and who also just happened to be a SmilesCorp spy. I couldn't believe it. What was he doing here?

Gordon Renfro stepped into the boiler room. Lucky for me, he didn't bother to turn on the light or he likely would have seen me. Instead he made straight for the corner.

Oh no, I thought.

He crouched and pulled aside the loose section of the baseboard.

No, no, no . . .

It made sense now. Of course it was Gordon Renfro who had taken photos of Hamstersaurus Rex and squirreled away a bunch of strange chemicals in a weird hole! But how did Wilbur Weber fit in to all of this? Were he and Renfro working together? What would a brilliant-yet-evil SmilesCorp scientist want with a sixth-grade snail enthusiast? And what about the weird little super-strong rodent in Wilbur's backpack? How did it fit in?

My questions would have to wait, though. I had more immediate concerns. Gordon Renfro dropped to his belly and reached inside the hole. For several long seconds I held my breath as I watched him groping around inside. I hoped against hope that Hammie Rex had the good sense to lie low. Of course, good sense had never been Hammie Rex's strong suit.

"EEEEEEEEEEEEEEEK!" shrieked Gordon Renfro as he yanked his hand out of the hole. Hamstersaurus Rex had chomped onto three of his fingers, and the little guy was holding on for dear life. Gordon Renfro squealed in pain and flapped his hand around like it was on fire. On the tenth or eleventh shake he finally managed to dislodge Hamstersaurus Rex, who went flying.

"Freeze, Renfro!" I yelled. "We got you surrounded, see!" (For some reason I'd lapsed into an old-timey cop voice.)

This startled Gordon Renfro, and he stumbled backward. There was a loud *klang!*—like a church bell getting rung with a glazed ham—as he smacked the back of his head on a metal pipe.

"Ow ow oweee!" he muttered, stumbling forward and clutching his head in pain. His ten-gallon hat was partially crumpled. By this time, Hamstersaurus Rex

KLANG!

had found his bearings and was ready to rejoin the fray. He did a flying hamster pounce and bit down hard on Gordon Renfro's butt.

"AAAAAAH-ha-ha-hawabagogga!" wailed Renfro, half running, half stumbling for the door. He practically tripped over that stupid fake beard twice on his way out. At the base of the stairs, he froze and turned to face me. "You may have won this round," he squealed in a grating, high-pitched voice, "but you haven't seen the last of us! Our plans will soon come to fruition! You'll see!"

Hamstersaurus Rex let loose a thunderous roar. Gordon Renfro slammed the door shut, and I heard him prop something against the outside, locking us into the boiler room. Hammie shook the UltraLite SmartShot off his head and charged. He hit the door headfirst like a battering ram. KALANG! It gave a little but didn't open. Outside I heard the sound of footsteps fading up the stairs. Gordon Renfro was getting away. Hammie backed up and ran at the door again. KALANG! It gave more this time, and I heard something crack on the other side. I stopped him.

"It's okay, buddy," I said. "He's gone. But I'm hoping we've got all the evidence we need."

I picked up the UltraLite SmartShot. Sure enough, the digital camera had kept filming the whole time.

I sat down to review the footage. First Hammie Rex surveyed the tunnel and the creepy chamber. Next a hand came groping in behind him (side note: Gordon Renfro really needed to clean under his nails. Blech). The hand grabbed the chemical canister near the entrance and started to pull it out of the tunnel. That's when Hamstersaurus Rex bit down on Renfro's fingers, and suddenly the footage became a nauseating POV Tilt-A-Whirl, as Hammie (and the camera) got slung around on the end of his flapping arm. I paused here. With his stupid fake beard askew, you could clearly make out Gordon Renfro's face. Nice!

I rewound the footage and watched it again. This time it wasn't for the purposes of investigation. It was for entertainment. All the sounds Gordon Renfro made were pretty funny ("AAAAAAH-ha-ha-hawabagogga"? Who yells that?). I rewound to watch it again, and something struck me. I paused the recording. Why was he reaching for that canister?

I showed Hammie Rex the tape and told him to retrieve the canister that Gordon Renfro was trying to grab from his little hidey-hole. Hammie barked and disappeared into the tunnel. He came back a minute later, rolling the canister with his nose.

"There's another rodent with superstrength," I said. "I bet it's more Huginex-G." That was the name of the proprietary SmilesCorp chemical that temporarily transformed a genetically modified squirrel into the behemoth Squirrel Kong.

I checked the label. Sure enough, the SmilesCorp logo was right there. But it wasn't Huginex-G. It was something called "PaleoGro." I'd never heard of it before.

"Well, if Gordon wants PaleoGro, that means he shouldn't have it," I said. I sent Hammie Rex back into the hole to clean out my classmates' missing items.

A couple more dino-strong head butts broke the three-legged chair Renfro had wedged under the knob to keep us trapped inside. I took Hamstersaurus Rex back into Meeting Club HQ.

"Nice work today, little guy," I said. "You deserve a treat." I reached into my backpack and pulled out a bag of Funchos Rockin' Hot Sauce and Chicken Noodle Flavor-Wedges (A SmilesCorp™ Product). Hamstersaurus Rex used to be uncontrollably addicted to junk food, but through the power of meditation, he had conquered his empty carb and artificial flavorings demons. Now he enjoyed them responsibly.

As the little guy ripped into the bag and gobbled down the salty snacks inside, I had a faint glimmer of hope. I didn't want to jinx it, but Hamstersaurus Rex hadn't moped in nearly an hour.

"Stay safe tonight. I'll see you tomorrow," I said. "Sleep tight!"

Hamstersaurus Rex froze. A look of utter sadness started to spread across his little face.

"What?" I said. "What did I say?"

Hammie Rex sighed and slumped forward, totally depressed once again.

"What? Was it because I said 'sleep'?"

Hammie Rex snorted pitifully.

"So I can't even say the word 'sleep' now, because it reminds you that Cartimandua fell asleep on your hamster date? Come on, Hammie!"

The little guy was still moaning as I shut the door. I shook my head and headed for home.

Back at my house, I popped the head off an old Tiny Wizards action figure and hid the Paleo-Gro canister inside the toy's hollow chest cavity. The canister was what Gordon Renfro went for first, so I figured it was the most important. Maybe Martha would know what PaleoGro was. I'd probably need to make peace with her first, though. I was crafting a sorry-ish sounding non-apology in my head when I heard a plink against my bedroom window.

I looked outside. There was a ninja standing in the bushes.

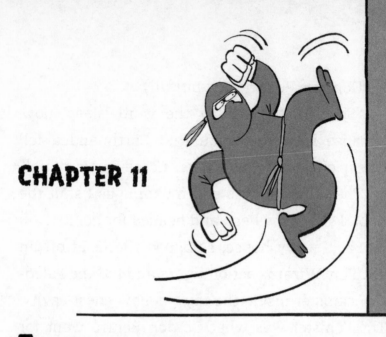

CHAPTER 11

POKED MY HEAD out the window. "Um, can I help you?" I said to the ninja.

"Ninja cartwheel!" yelled the ninja, and he did an awkward cartwheel that destroyed a good bit of my mom's tulip bed in the process. At the end of the acrobatic display, the ninja bowed and tried to pull off his mask. It was stuck. He struggled with it for a while.

"Need some help?" I asked.

"No. Shut up," muttered the ninja, still fighting with the mask. Finally, he succeeded in yanking it off with a loud ripping sound. "Bet you didn't know who I was," said Beefer Vanderkoff, panting.

"No idea," I said. "We get a lot of ninjas in this neighborhood."

"Well, you were always a little slow on the uptake, Sam," said Beefer. "Ninja parkour!" He ran at my house and tried to scale the wall up to my second-story bedroom window. Instead he sort of scrambled at the siding for a second and fell on his back with an "oof." After that, he just lay in the grass gazing up at the sky.

"If you want, we have stairs," I said.

My mom raised an eyebrow as she saw me let Beefer in the front door. "Hey, isn't that the kid who used to bully you?" she said.

"Yes, ma'am," said Beefer, before I could respond. "But Sam hasn't bullied me in quite a while, so I've decided to let bygones be bygones. When all is said and done, I think that deep down he's actually a good kid."

"Uh-huh," said my mom. "And why are you dressed like a mime?"

"Ninja," Beefer mumbled, now hanging his head in shame. "Makes more sense with the mask, except I washed it on hot instead of cold, and it shrank and I think I tore the inseam . . ."

"It's cool, Mom," I said. "Nothing to worry about."

My mom nodded and went back to watching her Norwegian detective show.

"So, what do you want?" I said to Beefer, once we were in my bedroom. I realized that came out a little harsh. I sometimes had trouble remembering that Beefer was no longer the goon who gave me daily swirlies. In the battle against Squirrel Kong, he'd even helped. "Hi, by the way," I added. There, that sounded a *little* bit friendlier.

"Don't try to butter me up," said Beefer, poking me in the chest. "You owe me!"

"Huh?"

"Remember how I single-handedly defeated that giant squirrel and saved the whole town?" said Beefer. "Maybe the world."

"You threw your snake at a little helicopter," I said.

"Well, anyway, crazy as it sounds, this time it's me that needs your help," said Beefer. He laughed to show how crazy it was.

"Ah, I think I know what this is about," I said. "It's called 'deodorant,' and yes, I can totally show you where they keep it at the pharmacy."

Beefer stopped laughing and stared at me. "Words hurt, Sam," he said.

"Huh. But I—I mean, okay. Sorry," I said. Whatever my new relationship with Beefer was, it would definitely take some getting used to.

"Look, I heard you're like a little junior kid detective now or something," said Beefer.

"Sort of," I said. "Today I solved the case of Dwight Feinberg's Missing Instant Camera."

"Don't care," said Beefer. "I have a real case for you. And it's a doozy. Who knows how deep this thing goes? Very mysterious cloak-and-diaper stuff."

"Cloak-and-*dagger*," I said.

Beefer turned pale. "You really think so? That's even worse."

"Look, just tell me what your case is and make it snappy," I said, pulling out my detective notebook.

"I'm being followed. Everywhere I go—home, school, the dojo, lute lessons—I keep seeing the same girl. I'm pretty sure she's either a member of a rival ninja clan or—and I don't want you to wet your little pants when I say this, Sam—*a werewolf*." Beefer paused for dramatic effect.

I sighed and started to put my notebook away.

"Hey, come on," said Beefer. "Don't you even want a description of the were-suspect?"

"Fine," I said, not really wanting a description of the were-suspect.

"She's got purple hair," said Beefer.

"Wait a second," I said, "I've seen her around, too. She was at Wilbur Weber's birthday party! In a SmilesCorp T-shirt!"

I quickly caught Beefer up on everything that had happened so far: the sabotaged RaddZone go-kart, the weird squealing rodent in Wilbur's backpack, and Gordon Renfro's creepy little hidey-hole/stalker shrine to Hammie Rex. Beefer stroked his chin, deep in thought.

"So Martha's still single?" he said.

"Huh?" I said. "I think you're focusing on the wrong part of the story. Look, man, the point is that if Gordon Renfro is back, it means SmilesCorp is at it again. I'm sure they're looking for—"

"Michael Perkins!" shrieked Beefer. "My beautiful bouncing baby boakeet!"

"I was going to say Hamstersarus Rex, on account of all the surveillance photos, but sure, maybe Michael Perkins, too," I said. "I bet Purple Hair is in cahoots on account of her shirt."

"Cahoots," said Beefer, shaking his head ominously.

"Look, Beefer, I'll help you try to find Purple Hair, but I'm going to need your help, too," I said. "That freaky little rodent is still on the loose. It must be one of the mutants that got set free when we broke into SmilesCorp. If you see or hear anything, let me know."

"All right," said Beefer. "Ninja shake." He stuck out his hand.

I shook it. "Deal," I said.

Beefer looked at me expectantly.

I sighed. "*Ninja* deal."

Now he smiled. "You know, Sam, I think it's pretty awesome that you went from being a bad guy to being a good guy."

"Come on!" I said.

"And now, in true ninja fashion, I must vanish without a trace." Beefer reached into his pockets and pulled out a smoke bomb and a lighter. He started trying to light it.

"Hey, hey, hey!" I yelled, slapping the smoke bomb out of his hands. "Don't do that in my house!"

"Can I do it in the yard?"

"I guess. But not near any of my mom's flowers."

A few minutes later, I looked out my window and saw Beefer standing on the front lawn. He lit the smoke bomb and ran away. It stained some of the grass blue.

The next day before school, I stood by the sixth-grade lockers and waited. Today was a landmark occasion for the Rex & Gibbs Detective Agency. We'd just closed our first four cases! Finally, I saw Tina Gomez walking down the hall, chatting with her friends.

"Hey, Tina, guess what I found," I said.

"Hmm," said Tina, "some sort of enchanted mask that can turn its wearer into any animal?"

"Uh . . . no," I said. "This." I held out her

worn-down eraser.

"What happened to it?" said Tina, crinkling her nose.

"I don't know," I said. "Somebody used it, I guess."

"Eh, you can keep it," said Tina. "I'll just get another one. They only cost, like, twenty-five cents, you know."

Before my head could explode, I saw Drew McCoy.

"Drew, my main man," I said, "I found your *Legend of Max Stomper* #338 gold-foil variant cover. Voilà!" I held up his comic book. A couple of pages fell out.

A look of horror spread across Drew's face. "The issue was mint," he said, flipping through it. "Max Stomper's face has been ripped out of every single page."

"You can still kind of tell what's going on," I said. "From what I gather, Max Stomper is often stomping."

"Sam, why did you show me this?" said Drew, now pale as a ghost. "What was once a thirty-nine-dollar collector's item is now a . . . a *human tragedy*." He walked off, shaking his head.

"I was trying to help," I said.

At this point I almost didn't want to find Dwight Feinberg. But I did.

"Hey, man. Here's your instant camera," I said, shoving it toward him with no fanfare.

"Thanks, but I already bought a new one," said Dwight. "And then I lost that one, too. Hey, maybe you can help me find it?"

"Sure," I said. "I'll keep my eyes peeled."

So far, solving cases hadn't been the thrill ride it was cracked up to be. Still, I knew one person who would be grateful for the result of my detective work.

"Missing something?" I said. I held out the Disc-whippers away jersey I'd recovered to Dylan.

"My jersey!" cried Dylan. "Oh man, now Coach Weekes won't have to kill me, except he kind of already wants to because I broke my ankle and basically tanked our whole season." She unfurled it: metallic mauve and purple, "D'AMATO 03" on the back. But I noticed that a little triangle of fabric had been snipped out of it. I frowned.

"Huh. Didn't see the hole before," I said.

"Don't worry, Sam, my dad can patch it," said Dylan. "So where was it?"

"In a weird tunnel," I said.

"A weird tunnel where the ghost of Horace Hotwater lives?" said Dylan, her eyes widening. "Well, 'lives' is the wrong word, but you know."

"Nope. The tunnel belongs to one Gordon Renfro, who's been creeping around like a total creep."

"Renfro!" said Dylan, pounding her fist into her palm. "That guy?!"

"Yep," I said. "He stole Dwight's camera to take spooky surveillance photos of Hammie Rex. You've got to see his new disguise. It makes the 'Todd Duderotti' ponytail-and-shades ensemble actually look subtle."

"Is Wilbur working for him?" said Dylan. "Do you think that's how he came by his evil steroid ferret or whatever?"

"Could be," I said. "Anyway, the good news is, there is no ghost."

Dylan frowned. "But I saw a jersey literally levitate, Sam. How could Gordon Renfro manage to pull that off?"

"Obviously with scientific . . . science," I said. "Because he's a scientist."

Dylan didn't look convinced.

"Okay, I'll admit Hamstersaurus Rex and I haven't pieced together all the clues yet," I said. "But this explains a lot. If Renfro's back in the picture—"

"Renfro's back in the picture!" said Martha, appearing out of nowhere like some sort of future-valedictorian/chameleon hybrid. "I'm going to redouble Cartimandua's security. From now on, she's going to be under twenty-four-hour video surveillance."

"I don't know if that's strictly necessary. But speaking of Cartimandua," I said, mentally reciting the words I had prepared in advance, "I want to express my deepest and most obligatory regrets that you somehow hurt your own feelings regarding Cartimandua being taken out of her cage for the sake of love et cetera and so forth."

Martha cocked her head.

"Masterful non-apology," said Dylan.

"Okay, fine," I said. "I'm sorry, Martha. Happy?"

"Apology accepted, Sam," said Martha, brightening. "You know, in the future, you should consider not doing anything wrong in the first place. Like me."

"I'll consider it," I said. "Anyway, now that that's out of the way, I need your help with something. Can you figure out what this is?" I handed her the action figure that had the PaleoGro hidden in its chest cavity.

"It's an action figure . . . which is *sort of* like a crude doll?" said Martha, holding it at arm's length. "I couldn't tell you much more than that. I don't really watch cartoons. I mostly stick to the nightly news."

"Don't let appearances fool you, Martha," I

said. "It's what's inside that counts." I popped the head off the Tiny Wizard and shook the PaleoGro canister out.

"PaleoGro?" said Dylan. "That sounds really familiar, but I can't remember why."

"That canister looks like it came from the school lab," said Martha. "We should return it."

"Not so fast," I said. "After Squirrel Kong destroyed the lab, it was remodeled to be totally state-of-the-art, right? Do you guys remember who paid for that?"

"SmilesCorp," said Dylan.

"And when Gordon Renfro was pretending to be Todd Duderotti," said Martha, "he was secretly using the new school lab as his home base to hunt down Squirrel Kong and Hamstersaurus Rex."

"Exactly," I said. "I think Renfro is back because he needs stuff from our school lab."

"But why can't he just get whatever he needs from SmilesCorp?" said Dylan.

"No idea," I said. "All I know is that he was willing to break into Horace Hotwater in a disguise to try to steal this canister of 'PaleoGro.'"

"I'll tell Elaine to change the locks on the lab door," said Martha.

"Elaine?" said Dylan.

"Oh, you would probably know her as Principal Truitt," said Martha.

Dylan shook her head.

"Good thinking, Martha," I said. "And can you try to figure out what PaleoGro is?"

"I'll do my best," said Martha. "Which is usually better than everyone else's." She pocketed the canister.

Dark thoughts of Gordon Renfro preoccupied me for the rest of the day. Yet again, Wilbur Weber didn't show up to school. I asked around to see if anybody had heard anything about him, but no one had. Turns out the kid didn't have many (non-snail) friends and nobody had seen him since the incident at RaddZone. Was he off regrouping with Gordon Renfro and his weird little animal friend? Were they plotting their next evil move? Another attack on Hamstersaurus Rex?

I was zoning out beside the good water fountain when Coach Weekes tapped me on the shoulder.

"How'd it work out?" he said.

"How did what work out?" I said.

"My Success Coaching for your sad 'friend'?" said Weekes, with several exaggerated winks and nudges and nose taps. "Because here's what I'm thinking: I could have a completely new career as an advice columnist. I already picked out the perfect name: *Goalkeeping with the Success Coach*." He stared at me expectantly for several seconds.

"It's a sports pun?" I said.

"See? I *knew* you'd get it and absolutely love it!" he cried, clapping me on the back. "Anyway, yeah, my thing is going to be to use a ton of sports puns and metaphors. For example, opportunity is like a football: when somebody tosses it your way, you just gotta hold on tight and run with it! And try to not get tackled. And go for the two-point conversion."

"Sounds like you've already put a lot of—"

"Got my resignation letter all typed up and ready to go!" He whipped out a folded sheet of paper and shoved it at me. "And you can be sure this bad boy has a few choice words for Principal

Truitt, too. That woman *never* gave me the knee-sock budget I requested. Not once."

"Whoa, whoa, whoa, Coach!" I said. "I think you might be getting a little ahead of yourself. Honestly, your advice didn't work out so well. My friend got out of his comfort zone and it was a disaster. Things are even worse than before. So."

"Hmm. Sounds like your quote-unquote 'friend' is really stuck behind the eight ball, success-wise. Another sports metaphor," said Coach Weekes, pocketing his letter of resignation. "Time for some advanced success coaching." He cracked his knuckles.

"Fine," I said. "Whatever you say."

"Success Coach's second rule: be direct!" said Coach Weekes. "Stop beating around the bush. Come right out and say what your goals are: *Give* me my knee-sock money! No, I *won't* pay for this floor-model toaster I broke! Yes, I *will* be an astronaut, even though I failed the physical exam and the background check! And so forth, et cetera, Gibbs."

"Uh-huh," I said.

Weekes's success coaching hadn't gotten

Hammie anywhere before. In fact, it was so wrong, it was basically the opposite of right. That got me thinking. What if Hammie did the opposite of what Success Coach said this time? Instead of being direct, he could be indirect. Mysterious, even! What if Cartimandua received a nice, thoughtful gift from a "secret admirer"? Maybe that could add a little bit of excitement and turn this whole catastrophe around. What to get her, though? I knew Cartimandua liked lettuce.

On my way to lunch, I swung by Meeting Club HQ and collected a despondent Hamstersaurus Rex. I ran the plan by him, and he didn't object (or react in any way other than to frown). So I tucked him into my shirt pocket and headed to the cafeteria.

"Hi, can I have some lettuce?" I said to Judy, the lunch lady.

"I got six types of lettuce," she said, crossing her arms. "You're going to have to be more specific."

"Give me all of them," I said.

Now she was doubly suspicious. "How come?"

"What can I say?" I said. "I'm a lettuce head!"

Somehow she was persuaded. I took all six

types of lettuce and arranged them into a beautiful lettuce-y bouquet, which I tied with a ribbon that was actually tape. Then I filled out a card. "To: Cartimandua. From: Anonymous. Please enjoy this lettuce." Hmm. It needed a little something more. At the bottom I wrote, "Best of luck in all your future endeavors" like I'd seen on a greeting card once. Perfect!

Hammie peeked out of my pocket and watched me express his heartfelt and poetic sentiment and attach it to his extremely thoughtful gift. "She's going to love this, buddy," I whispered to him. "Nice work!" I hurried back to our classroom before lunch was over.

I found Mr. Copeland reclining in his swivel chair. He suddenly snapped awake.

"Please don't tow my car!" he screamed. Mr. Copeland looked around and gathered himself.

"Just resting my eyes. Wait, what are you even doing here, Sam? It's lunchtime."

"I'm here to deliver this lettuce bouquet to Cartimandua!" I triumphantly showed it to him.

"Seventeen years of teaching and I've never had a class that was this into hamsters," said Mr. Copeland, shaking his head. "Anyway, don't let me stop you." He gestured toward the hamster cage.

Cartimandua was inside, licking a stray piece of lint. I opened the little door to the PETCATRAZ Pro™.

"Why, hello, Cartimandua," I said. "I have a special gift from a secret admirer." I gave her the lettuce. "Pretty artfully arranged, huh? The romaine makes a nice contrast with iceberg, I find."

She sniffed at the bouquet. Then she nibbled a little bit.

"So far, so good," I whispered to Hammie Rex in my pocket. I felt him stir.

Cartimandua ate more lettuce. She clearly loved her gift.

"Well," I said, backing toward the door. "I'll

just leave you to think about how thoughtful this amazing gift is and wonder who the mysterious and handsome—"

Cartimandua barfed everywhere.

"Yikes!" said Mr. Copeland, looking up from his yogurt cup. "Is that normal?"

"Um," I said. "I thought she liked lettuce?"

"How should I know?" said Mr. Copeland. "Sam, if you poisoned the new hamster, Martha's never going to let me hear the end of it!"

"Good idea!" I cried. "Martha!"

Cartimandua barfed again. I picked her up and ran.

"Make way! Coming through!" I cried as I carried Cartimandua ahead of me down the hall. "Hamster horking over here!"

"Whoa, what's wrong with Carabiner?" said Omar Powell, jumping back as I rushed past.

"Cartagena looks sick," offered Julie Bailey helpfully.

Cartimandua threw up twice more by the time I found Martha on her way back from lunch.

"Sam, what happened?" cried Martha, snatching

Cartimandua away from me. "This is Hamster Code Red!"

"Uh. Looks like somebody gave her this." I held out the limp, chewed-up lettuce bouquet.

"Somebody?" said Martha as she pulled a stethoscope out of her backpack and started to monitor Cartimandua's heart rate. "Who?"

"Well, it says it's from 'Anonymous,' so there's really no way to prove—"

Martha grabbed the card. "It's your hand-writing."

"Okay, technically, yes, it is my handwriting," I said. "But you said she likes lettuce!"

"I said she likes lettuce *in moderation*!" cried Martha as she strapped a tiny blood pressure cuff on Cartimandua's front leg. "This is way, *way* too much lettuce for her! Cartimandua has a very sensitive digestive tract. You would know that if you ever bothered to read her medical history file."

"It was seventy-five pages long!" I said. "I got tired of reading about a genetic history of gingivitis on her father's side!"

Martha glared at me.

"Sorry. I'll read it. I promise," I said. "Is she going to be okay?"

Martha paused to read the tiny gauge on the miniature blood pressure cuff. "Luckily, yes," she said. "But this is your final warning, Sam. Stop trying to play hamster matchmaker. It's been a disaster."

"Hey, I'm just trying to help my little friend," I said. "He's depressed. He lies facedown on the floor all day long. He's barely been eating. He's basically lost the urge to smash things."

"Hamstersaurus Rex has brought nothing but trouble to Cartimandua," said Martha.

"Okay, you have a point," I said. "But ultimately isn't it better to have loved and barfed than never to—"

"Sam, she obviously doesn't even like him anyway!" said Martha.

I could feel the little guy wince inside my pocket as she said it. Before I could reply, there was a tap on my shoulder.

"Uh, Sam," said Jared Kopernik. He was

standing sheepishly behind me with his hands behind his back.

"Not now, Jared," I said.

"Sam, seriously," said Jared, "I think you'll want to read this." He handed me an envelope and walked off.

Martha and I called a time-out on our argument. She watched over my shoulder as I opened the envelope. Inside was a folded piece of paper. It read: "I owe you an apology. Meet me at my house after school." At the bottom, it was signed "Wilbur Weber."

CHAPTER 12

AFTER SCHOOL, I headed to Wilbur's house with Hamstersaurus Rex in tow. Did he really intend to explain himself and let bygones be bygones? Or was this a Gordon Renfro/Smiles-Corp trap? Was I walking into some sort of final, epic showdown? Wilbur's creepy rodent beast against my dino-hamster, mutant versus mutant.

Unfortunately, I seriously doubted Hamstersaurus Rex had the will to fight. He was limp as cooked pasta, sniffling in my pocket and not doing much else. I was never sure how much Hammie understood when people spoke, but somehow he'd gotten the gist of what Martha was saying: he and Cartimandua weren't meant to be. He was at least eight times more depressed than before. Oh, how I longed for the days of continuous moaning. Now even moaning was too much effort for him.

So I brought Dylan along for extra backup. Normally she was tough and capable. But today she wasn't operating at 100 percent either. For one thing, she was on crutches, so the walk to Wilbur's house was extra slow. For another, she still hadn't gotten over the idea that she was somehow supernaturally cursed.

"I'm worried, Sam," said Dylan. "You say that there is no ghost and it's just Gordon Renfro's weird plans. But I still feel, like, a sense of doom. Ill omens. Dark portents. Like today's the day something really bad is going to happen." She shivered.

"Stop it with that stuff," I said. "You can hang back. Maintain an element of surprise. If you see anybody suspicious, hit 'em where it hurts. Maybe I won't even need your help."

We turned on to Walnutwood Court, where

Wilbur lived. On the opposite side of the street was a pile of leaves that had been raked extra high by one of his neigh-bors. Dylan decided it was a good place to hide for a surprise attack.

"All right, buddy," I said to Hammie Rex. "Look alive." He didn't.

I knocked on the door of Number 186 and waited. My pulse was pounding, my adrenaline pumping.

"Can I help you?" said a man who looked like an owl in a sport coat, presumably Wilbur's father.

"Um, yes," I said. "I'm here to see Wilbur."

"Oh, he doesn't exist," said Wilbur's dad, "at least socially. You see, he's been grounded for—well, basically *forever*. In fact, I wish there was a stronger word than 'grounded' that could more accurately describe my son's current status.

'Buried,' maybe? Anyway, short answer: no, you can't see him."

"It's actually important," I said.

"Uh-huh," said Mr. Weber. "Well, he'll be graduating from the Colonel Aldous Buchan Military Academy for Boys in approximately six years. Hopefully it can wait." Mr. Weber started to close the door.

"Is he in trouble because of what happened at RaddZone?" I asked.

"Why, yes, he is," said Mr. Weber. "My wife and I thought we raised a kind, responsible young man. I'm afraid we were sorely mistaken. Goodbye . . . um, I'm afraid I didn't catch your name."

"Sam Gibbs," I said. "I'm actually the kid whose go-kart he sabotaged. And I'm here because— because he offered me an apology."

Mr. Weber paused. He nodded. "And so you deserve one. Please come inside," he said. "Wilbur's room is upstairs."

It wasn't hard to figure out which door was his. It had a large sign that said "MAKE WAY FOR SNAILS!" in block letters.

If this was a trap, I wasn't going to get caught flat-footed. It would be me who made the first move, put Wilbur on the defensive. I took a deep breath. Then I kicked open the door.

"Hamstersaurus Rex Super Prehistoric Mega-Dino Hurricane Attack!" I yelled as I ran in, waving Hamstersaurus Rex around in front of me like a hand grenade. Hammie Rex sniffled.

My surprise battle cry was enough to startle Wilbur, though, who shrieked and fell off his bed. Inside, the room was dimly lit. The curtains were pulled and the walls were lined with terrariums containing hundreds, if not thousands, of snails.

Wilbur popped up, his eyes wide.

"Sam, if you're still mad about RaddZone," said Wilbur, "I honestly don't remember what happened there!"

"Well, you said you'd explain everything," I said, brandishing an unenthusiastic Hammie in his general direction. "So get to it!"

"That is everything!" said Wilbur. "In fact, I don't remember anything for the two whole days before it happened. You see, I was out taking Mr. Football for a walk one morning—"

"Mr. Football?" I said, looking in the terrariums. "Is that the name of the furry little mutant you had in your backpack?"

"Furry? Heavens, no!" said Wilbur. "This is Mr. Football." He held up a glistening snail the size of a bagel.

"Blech," I said, involuntarily stepping backward. "That thing's getting slime all over you."

"That's how I know he loves me," he said. "Even if he's the only one." Wilbur blinked back tears and gave Mr. Football a tender kiss on his head. (Actually, I'm not sure if snails have heads.

The part where the eyes come out? Anyway, I repeat: blech.)

"Look, I don't have time for snail smooches," I said. "If this is some sort of ambush or trap, why don't you just do it already?"

"It's not a trap," said Wilbur, who was now full-on sobbing as he cuddled Mr. Football close. "You keep saying that I had a furry animal in my backpack. But you've known me for years. Can you honestly imagine me, Wilbur Weber, having a pet that isn't snails? Look at my room!"

Definitely full of snails. There were snail posters on the walls. It smelled like snails. (Blech.)

"It is kind of hard to imagine," I admitted. I lowered Hamstersaurus Rex.

Wilbur dried his eyes. "Sam, my mind is all . . . scrambled. Nothing makes sense."

"Just tell me how Gordon Renfro fits into all of this," I said.

"Gordon who?"

"Todd Duderotti! Our old science teacher," I said. "The ponytail guy!"

"He seemed cool," said Wilbur with a shrug.

"But I haven't seen him since he stopped coming to school."

"He has a hidey-hole full of stolen stuff in the school basement," I said. "Strange chemicals! Creepy pictures of Hamstersaurus Rex!"

Wilbur squinted and rubbed his head like he had a headache. "I kind of remember something like that. Maybe?"

"What about the PaleoGro?"

"Yeah, wait . . . that rings a bell," said Wilbur. "He looked into my eyes and told me he needed a bunch of chemicals from the school science lab. PaleoGro was the most important . . ."

"Who looked into your eyes?" I said. "Who wanted you to get it? Was it a guy in a dumb cowboy hat and a ridiculous beard? *Who?*"

Wilbur had gone pale. He blinked and rubbed his temples. "I—I don't know. I'm sorry, Sam. Every time I try to think too hard about it, I get a headache. But I know you'll get to the bottom of this, 'cause you're an ace detective. And then you can prove to my mom and dad that it wasn't my fault and they don't need to send me to the Colonel

Aldous Buchan Military Academy for Boys." His eyes welled with tears again. "They have a strict 'no snails' policy." He burst out crying.

I sighed. "All right, man. I'll do my best. Sorry I threatened you with a Hamstersaurus Rex Super Prehistoric Mega-Dino Hurricane Attack. I was obviously bluffing." I held up a despondent Hamstersaurus Rex, who practically oozed through my fingers. "Anyway, if you remember anything else, please contact me."

He nodded and planted another wet one on Mr. Football. Blech. Blech. Blech.

"And thanks for the note," I said.

Wilbur looked at me. "Note? What note?"

CHAPTER 13

MY JAW DROPPED. I pulled the note out of my pocket and showed Wilbur.

"Yeah, that's not my handwriting," he said as he stroked Mr. Football. "I always dot my i's with little snails."

"Jared Kopernik!" I cried.

My mind raced. Jared had intentionally lured me to Wilbur's house with a fake note? Then Jared must be in on it with Gordon Renfro, too—whatever "it" was! If he wanted me here, that meant he *didn't* want me somewhere else.

Without another word I turned and ran for the front door.

Snails

Wilbur's words now echoed in my head: *He looked into my eyes and told me he needed a bunch of chemicals from the school science lab.*

I had to get back to Horace Hotwater Middle School as soon as possible—before Gordon Renfro could get his hands on any more of the ingredients he needed for whatever evil he was planning!

As I burst out of the Webers' front door and out onto their porch, I nearly smacked right into the girl with the purple hair. I skidded to a halt and we stared at each other for a half second. She opened her mouth and reached into her messenger bag—

THWANG! A disc-golf disc ricocheted off the side of Purple Hair's head.

"Nailed her!" cried Dylan, standing in a pile of leaves from across the street.

Stunned, the purple-haired girl turned and bolted.

"Wait!" I cried. "Hammie, don't let her get away!" I tossed the little guy onto the ground. Hammie let out a long sigh and turned to gaze forlornly at a wilting flower in Wilbur's yard.

"Are you kidding me?!" I cried.

By now, Purple Hair was halfway down the block. Man, she was fast! There was no way I was going to catch her, and neither was Dylan, stuck on her crutches. Suddenly a shadowy figure leaped across her path.

"And so the hunter becomes the hunted," said Beefer Vanderkoff, clad in full ninja garb. "Wombat style!" He struck a bizarre martial arts pose that, for the sake of argument, I'll say looked a teensy bit like a wombat.

"Move!" cried Purple Hair without slowing down.

"'Fraid not, sister," said Beefer. "You. Shall. Not. P—" Without missing a step, the purple-haired girl kicked him in the gut and kept on running. With a soft murmur, Beefer went down like a sack of laundry. Purple Hair disappeared around the corner. By the time I got to Beefer a few seconds later, he could almost talk again.

"Did . . . she . . . pass?" he wheezed from the ground.

"And how," I said. "But this doesn't feel right. I think she's trying to distract us from the school lab. I need to get back there, ASAP!"

"All right, I'll handle Purple Hair," said Beefer, pushing himself up off the ground. "And this time I won't go so easy on her . . . which I did intentionally. That's what happened." He jogged after her, clutching his gut.

I grabbed Hamstersaurus Rex, who was still contemplating that tragic wilted flower, and Dylan and I set off in the direction of school as fast as we could.

The front door to Horace Hotwater Middle School was ajar when we got back.

"Not good," I said. "We might be too late."

"Sorry, Sam," said Dylan. "I wish I could go faster on these stupid crutches. Ugh." Dylan started to throw them before she realized that would be a terrible idea.

"We might still have a chance to stop Renfro," I said. "You ready?"

"Yeah," said Dylan. She lowered her voice. "But what about him?"

Hamstersaurus Rex was still sobbing quietly. It was time for me to make a decision. I took the little guy aside. "All right, Hammie ol' buddy, maybe it's best if you hang back for this one, okay? For your own safety. Just until you're in a better place emotionally."

I never thought there would come a day when I would leave Hamstersaurus Rex behind on an adventure. But I did. And he didn't even seem to care; no reverse psychology this time. I left the little guy in an existential funk by the door, and Dylan and I headed inside.

The school was dark and quiet. The only sound was the faint hum of the air-conditioning and the squeak of our sneakers on freshly mopped linoleum. As quietly as we could, we made for the science lab.

When we got there, we found the door closed

and locked. There weren't any obvious signs of a break-in. Dylan and I peered through the window. It was dark, but I didn't see anyone inside.

"Nobody here," said Dylan.

"So where are they?" I said.

I felt an eerie, now-familiar sensation come over me. It was the same feeling I'd had before, when the bulletin board had ripped itself off the wall and flown at my head.

"Sam, what's happening?" said Dylan. She raised her arm. The hairs on it were standing straight up.

"Something bad," I said.

Suddenly, the trophy case nearby began to rattle and shake. A twenty-year-old district championship diving cup smacked against the glass and made a spiderweb crack. Dylan and I started to run. A potted plant whipped across the floor ahead of us and smashed against the wall in an explosion of dirt and crockery.

"Sam, how did that—"

BANG! I nearly hit the ground at the volume of the noise.

BANG! . . . BANG! . . . BANG! We turned. It was the wall of lockers nearby. Their doors were opening and slamming shut of their own accord.

Dylan's face had lost all color now. She was trembling, and her voice was barely a whisper. "*It's him,*" she said. "*It's the ghost of Horace Hotwater.*"

Dylan turned and fled as fast as she could. I couldn't blame her. In fact, following seemed like a pretty nifty idea. But I didn't. Instead a strange sense of resolve came over me. Scared as I might be, I knew where I had to go. Pencils and loose notebook paper and other bits of garbage swirled through the air around me as I walked toward Mr. Copeland's classroom.

Of course, Gordon Renfro was waiting there for me. He stood outside the door, still wearing his ridiculous beard and cowboy hat. If I hadn't been terrified beyond all reason, I would have laughed.

"Greetings," said Renfro in that same awful, high-pitched voice. "We have been expecting you. But where is the 'Hamster Hero of Horace Hotwater' that everyone finds *soooo* delightful?"

"None of your business, Renfro!" I cried. "He

doesn't belong to SmilesCorp. And whatever you're up to, it's not going to work."

He giggled. "We are not Renfro," he said. "But since you mention our plans, they do, in fact, require the PaleoGro you stole from us. Give it back. Now."

"Don't have it," I said. "Why do you even *want* it anyway?"

"Oh, you'll learn soon enough," said Renfro, still giggling. "But first I will need you to open Cartimandua's cage."

". . . Cartimandua?" I said, baffled. "Why bring her into this? She's just a normal civilian hamster. It's a free country. Go to a pet store and buy your own, Renfro. Leave Hamstersaurus Rex and Cartimandua alone!"

"I told you," said Gordon Renfro, "we are not Renfro." Slowly his cowboy hat began to float off his head all on its own. "Renfro is but a puppet. *We are the Mind Mole!*"

The hat continued to float upward until it was a foot above his scalp. But that wasn't the weirdest thing.

On top of Renfro's bald spot, there was a weird-looking mole with an oversized head, wearing a tiny purple cape—the swatch cut out of Dylan's jersey. The mole's beady eyes flashed, and instantly I recognized them.

Those eyes . . . those strange little eyes . . .

CHAPTER 14

"THE MIND MOLE!" I screamed in terror.

The entire sixth-grade class was staring at me, aghast, including Mr. Copeland.

"Well, that's an interesting guess, Sam," said Mr. Copeland, frowning. "But I'm afraid the correct answer is 'a rectangle.' Your response *does* raise some bigger questions about what I'm doing with my life, when I could, for instance, still be giving ocean kayaking lessons on the big island of Hawaii."

My mouth was dry. I was disoriented. Why was I in class? Where was Gordon Renfro? Where was the horrible mole with the giant head? Was it all a dream? If it was all a dream, that would be *so lame!*

"Perhaps I'll contemplate my own life choices while Martha *yet again* addresses the entire class," said Mr. Copeland. "I'm going to guess it's about hamsters."

Martha nodded gravely.

"Take it away, Martha," said Mr. Copeland, and he quietly put his head on his desk.

Martha stood and faced the class. "Unfortunately," she said, "I have no updates on the pending investigation into the disappearance of our beloved class pet."

Was Hamstersaurus Rex missing again? I turned to face the back of the classroom. Sure enough, the PETCATRAZ Pro™ was empty, its little door swinging open on its hinges. But wait, it wasn't Hamstersaurus Rex who lived there anymore. It was Cartimandua now, wasn't it?

"I know these last four days have been hard, but please, dear classmates, do not give up hope," said Martha, her stony expression threatening to crack. "That's not what Cartimandua would want you to do. I remain confident she will be returned safe and sound." And with that she gave me the evil eye.

Huh? What did I do? Wait, did she just say *four days?* How could that be possible? I wondered. It was only seconds earlier that Gordon Renfro had told me to open her cage. That was who took Cartimandua: Gordon Renfro and the Mind Mole!

The bell for lunch rang, and we all stood to file out of the classroom.

"Martha!" I said. "I know exactly who—"

"Back off, Sam!" snapped Martha. "I'm not giving it to you, okay? I don't know what you want it for, but I'm sure it's nothing good."

I was stunned. "Give *what* to me?"

Martha looked around to make sure no one was else was listening. "The PaleoGro."

"Huh? I gave it to *you* to figure out what it was," I said. "I don't want the PaleoGro!"

"Oh really?" she said, putting her hands on her hips. "Then why have you been sneaking around my house at night trying to steal it back? Don't act like you weren't!"

I was dumbfounded. I had no idea what to say. Had Martha completely lost it? Or had I?

"I'm really confused right now," I said.

"Well, things are crystal clear to me," said Martha. She squinted as a group of our classmates approached. "I don't have time for whatever you're trying to pull, Sam. Now are you ready to do what we discussed?"

"What did we . . . discuss?"

"Returning the, ahem, *item* you already took," said Martha, gritting her teeth. "This is your last chance, Sam. Or I really tell Principal Truitt."

"But I didn't *steal* anything!"

"Liar!" cried Martha as she stalked off toward the cafeteria.

I had no idea what to make of any of this. Martha and I should have been working together to get Cartimandua back. We were a Hamster Monitor team! Instead she seemed to think I was another villain in the story.

To make matters more annoying, Coach Weekes happened to catch the look on my face.

"Why the scowl, Gibbs?" said Weekes. "Success

Coach's third rule: never frown! Always keep a crazy smile plastered on your face, even when you're completely miserable. If you *appear* happy, others will—"

"Great idea, Coach!" I snapped as I continued down the hall.

His unwanted success-coaching jogged my memory, though: if I looked bummed out, Hammie must be truly heartbroken that Cartimandua was missing. Wait, where *was* Hamstersaurus Rex? I'd left him by the door of the school, but then . . .

I turned and ran for Meeting Club HQ. The little closet was empty, save for the stacks of unwanted books. There were thirty-five hardcover copies of *Doorknobs Are Cool!* but no Hamstersaurus Rex.

At lunch I found Dylan. Maybe she could offer some explanation as to what the heck was happening.

"Dylan, I feel like I'm going

nuts," I said, setting my tray down beside hers.

"Oh," said Dylan, mashing at her peas with a fork.

"Oh?" I said. "Your best friend confides that he might be losing his marbles and all you can say is 'Oh'?"

Dylan gave me a pained look. "That's too bad . . . that you're going nuts."

"Yeah, it is too bad," I said. "Don't tell me you hate me now, too!"

"I don't hate you!" said Dylan. "I thought you hated me."

"What? Of course not!" I said. "Why?"

"Because you didn't talk to me for, like, four whole days!"

"I didn't?"

"No!" said Dylan. "You acted like I didn't exist. Not a single word."

"Well, about that—"

"Look, I'm sorry that I chickened out," said Dylan. "If I hadn't, maybe I could have stopped whatever happened from happening. I'm useless." Dylan stared at the floor.

"You're not useless," I said. "I need you, pal. Now more than ever."

"Really?"

"Even more than when that pail was stuck on my head in preschool," I said.

Dylan took a deep breath and nodded. "Okay, Sam," she said. "I'll do it for you. And I promise I won't chicken out and let you down again. So what's the plan?"

"I know who kidnapped Cartimandua," I said. "But Martha won't listen to me. I need you to intervene on my behalf. Get her to believe me."

We found Martha sitting by herself as she ate her beet salad. I kept a safe distance while Dylan tried to talk to her.

"Look, I know you're pretty angry right now," said Dylan. "But you *need* to know who kidnapped Cartimandua."

"Oh, I already do know who kidnapped Cartimandua," said Martha.

"You do?" said Dylan.

"Of course," said Martha. "It was Sam."

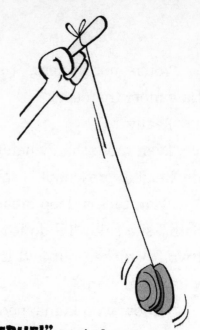

CHAPTER 15

"THAT'S NOT TRUE!"** I cried.

"Oh, isn't it?" said Martha. "Because I have incontrovertible proof that you're the guilty party. And since your vocabularies are smaller than mine, I'll just tell you, 'incontrovertible' means it can't be disputed."

"What?" I said. "Come on, Martha! I'm a Hamster Monitor! The ridiculous oath I took means something! I don't even get what's happening—"

"Easy, Sam," said Dylan, putting a hand on my chest. "What proof do you have, Martha?"

Martha pulled out an UltraLite SmartShot Mini. For a split second I was overcome with

AV jealousy—the new Mini is sooo small—until I remembered I was on trial here for a crime I didn't commit. Martha flipped open the LCD display and cued up some footage. Then she turned the screen so we could see.

"Remember how I said I was going to keep Cartimandua under twenty-four-hour video surveillance?" said Martha.

"I thought you were kidding," I said.

"I'm never kidding," said Martha.

The camera showed our sixth-grade classroom in the familiar tones of night-vision green. Specifically, it was pointed right at Cartimandua's cage. In the corner it was time-stamped four days earlier at 6:07 p.m.

"You set up a hidden camera in our classroom?" said Dylan. "That's kinda creepy."

"I have six hidden cameras in our classroom," said Martha. "And creepiness is the price we pay for law and order! Anyway, just watch."

At 6:08 p.m., a familiar figure walked into frame. He opened the cage, took Cartimandua out, and walked back toward the door. It was me.

"Want to watch it again?" said Martha.

"No," I said. "That's—that's—it can't . . ." I trailed off. My mind was reeling. I couldn't believe my eyes.

Dylan backed away from me like I was poison. "Sam, what were you thinking?" she whispered. "Why did you do it?"

"It's not what it looks like," I said.

Martha looked like she actually might hit me. "So I guess Cartimandua and Hamstersaurus went on another 'hamster date' or something?" she said. "That's why you kidnapped her? Or do you still want to make the ludicrous argument that it isn't you on the tape? By the way, 'ludicrous' means—"

"No, it's clearly me on the tape," I said. I took a deep breath. "Guys, I know this is going to be one of the weirder things I've ever said, but . . . I'm pretty sure I was mind-controlled. By a mole."

I'm not gonna lie, it was a hard sell. It took a long time to convince them both that I was neither crazy nor evil. But eventually I did it. Real friends believe you (that's one of the best things about them). By the time the lunch bell rang,

Martha and Dylan were ready to help me take on the evil Mind Mole and save Cartimandua and Hamstersaurus Rex.

On the way back to class, we caught up with Jared Kopernik in the hall.

"Hey, Jared," I said. "Were you, by any chance, recently brainwashed by an evil mole with a massive head?"

Jared looked at me like I was insane. It was the way most people looked at him most of the time. "Hmm," he said. "Not to my knowledge, no."

"Think back," I said. "Do you remember staring into a pair of creepy little mole eyes? And then waking up a couple of days later in a weird place?"

"Wait," said Jared, clutching his head with both hands. "Yeah, I do kind of remember something like that. I was out behind the abandoned inner-tube factory looking for UFOs when I saw something skitter behind a pile of rusty old Schrader valves. I thought it might be a baby Bigfoot—this is their migratory season— so I went to check it out.

I peeked over the pile, and then I remember seeing those . . . eyes. And then, WHAM! It's two days later and I'm eating dinner with my folks."

Jared couldn't remember much more than that, but he seemed really disappointed he hadn't been abducted by extraterrestrials or even Bigfoots. (Bigfeet?)

Martha, Dylan, and I huddled.

"It sounds like you're on the right track, Sam," said Dylan. "So this big-brained mole is another SmilesCorp mutant?"

"And he's even deadlier than Squirrel Kong because he can hypnotize people," said Martha, taking rapid notes in perfect cursive.

"Yep," I said. "In fact, I don't think any of this is Gordon Renfro's plan at all. The Mind Mole called him 'a puppet.' He's just another victim, like Wilbur, Jared, and me!"

"Makes me almost feel sorry for the guy," said Dylan. "Almost."

"From the incidents you described," said Martha, "it also sounds like the Mind Mole is capable of moving objects around by just thinking about it."

"Telekinesis!" said Dylan, pounding her fist into her palm. "That explains the floating jersey."

"And the bulletin board that attacked me, and the Ms. Super Plunger Jr. game that almost flattened me and pretty much everything else," I said.

"So there really wasn't a ghost after all?" said Dylan. She looked mightily embarrassed.

"No, ghosts aren't real, Dylan," said Martha.

"Oh, and moles with paranormal mental powers are?!" said Dylan.

"Obviously," said Martha.

"So we know the Mind Mole abducted Cartimandua, but what about Hammie?" I said.

"When Cartimandua went missing, I looked for him," said Martha. "He hasn't been in his little weird-smelling closet since you got hypnotized."

"Meeting Club Headquarters," I corrected her.

"I hate to say it," said Dylan, "but maybe the Mind Mole got Hammie Rex, too."

"I hope not," I said. "But when I left him, I'm afraid he was feeling pretty 'emo.' Certainly in no condition to put up a fight."

"Then that's one more missing hamster we need to add to the Hamster Monitor hamster docket!" cried Martha.

That afternoon, Dylan, Martha, and I looked high and low for any sign of Hamstersaurus Rex (Martha even bailed on her competitive origami team practice, so I knew it was serious). We checked and rechecked everywhere he might be: Meeting Club HQ, the cafeteria, Mr. Copeland's room, the athletic fields, and the woods behind the school where Hammie and I sometimes shot our movies. We even checked my garage at home just in case he'd somehow made his way back there. We didn't find him.

Outside, the sun was setting as we sat in my room, exhausted from our search. My mom brought us a plate of oatmeal raisin cookies. They didn't make anyone feel better.

"Don't worry, Sam," said Dylan. "We'll find the little guy."

"And we'll find Cartimandua, too," said Martha. "A Hamster Monitor Always Gets Her Hamster. That's our motto. I just it made up, but I think it's good. How would you guys feel about sleeve patches that say that on—"

"Wait," I said. "Maybe we *already* know where Cartimandua is. I mean, maybe I do."

"Explain," said Dylan.

"Well, I'm the one who kidnapped Cartimandua, so I must know where I took her. Right?"

"But you don't remember anything about the time you were under the Mind Mole's mole-control," said Dylan.

"Maybe deep down, I do?" I said.

"Right!" said Martha. "The information could still be buried in your subconscious. I could hypnotize you!"

"Tap the brakes," I said, backing away. "I'm not so sure that's—"

"Don't worry, I have a technique that I learned at Magician Camp two summers ago," said Martha. "It's utterly safe. I got hypnotized there dozens of times, and look at me. *I'm perfectly normal.*"

I didn't know how to respond.

"As crazy as things have gotten, maybe it's our best option," said Dylan. "If hypnosis can help us find Cartimandua, then maybe it can lead us to Hamstersaurus Rex, too."

"Fine," I said. "But I better not wake up interested in antique dolls."

"Excelsior!" said Martha. "Now, does anyone have a pocket watch?"

"Sure," said Dylan. "I just got three for my ninety-fifth birthday."

Martha cocked her head. "I thought you were twelve," she said.

"It was sarcasm, Martha. You're going to love it someday," I said as I grabbed a yo-yo off the floor. "Would this work instead?"

"Perfectly," said Martha. She dangled the yo-yo in front of my face, slowly swinging it back and forth, like the pendulum of a grandfather clock. "Sam, I want you to relax. Imagine you're in a very safe, calming place. Perhaps in a classroom, taking a high-school-level math test. Or maybe reviewing your permanent record with the secretary general of the United Nations—"

"How about I'm in a hammock?" I said.

"Okay," said Martha, "you're taking a

high-school-level math test in a hammock—"

"No, no, just sitting in a hammock. Doing nothing," I said. "And Hammie Rex is there, too, and he's also doing nothing."

"Suit yourself; seems like a waste of time," said Martha. She shrugged. "Anyway, I want you to focus on my voice to visualize that hammock. Feel the breeze on your face. Breathe in the smell of fresh-cut grass. Hear the rhythmic cadence of Hamstersaurus Rex dripping drool. Plink. Plink. Plink. Every muscle is starting to loosen. The tension is leaving your body. Your breathing is slowing down . . . I'm going to count backward from forty-seven, and when I reach one, you're going to find yourself in a deep, deep hypnotic state. You will not awaken from this hypnotic state until I say the phrase 'Punctuality is preferred,' okay?"

"Sounds great," I said.

"Okay," said Martha. "Forty-seven . . . forty-six . . ."

As she spoke, I began to feel calmer and calmer. Drowsy, even. I yawned. It was a very comfy imaginary hammock. And Hamstersaurus Rex was right there beside me, warming his scaly belly in the summer sun. I scratched under his chin, and the little guy belched. Martha's voice had faded to a to a distant, pleasant drone.

". . . three . . . two . . . one," said Martha. "Now, Sam, I want you to think back to four days earlier. Remember where you went, what you did . . ."

Just like on the video, I remembered walking into the classroom, unlocking Cartimandua's cage, and carrying her out of the school. I walked through the town of Maple Bluffs, crossing parking lots and lawns, streets and fields, and at some point, a golf course. People waved to me, and I didn't wave back. I knew where I was going. And at last, I found myself standing before a nondescript strip mall. On one side was a Coat Barn. On the other was Harry's Health Food Hut.

"I want you to tell me where you took Cartimandua" came Martha's pleasant voice, now a faint echo, as I somehow wandered through my own memories.

The windows had been blacked out so that I couldn't see inside. I heard the rasp of the lock, and I pushed through a door and into a darkened lobby. It was piled high with the big rolls of the butcher paper that had been used to block all sunlight from the outside world. There were stacks of empty crates marked "Grade AAA Premium Earthworms" and "Billy's Bait Shop Bulk Beetles." (Mole food, I realized.) I handed Cartimandua off to a shadowy figure. He had the grinning face of Gomer Gopher. I knew where I had taken the poor hamster.

"RaddZone," I said.

"Punctuality is preferred," said Martha.

Instantly, I felt clearheaded and alert.

"So Cartimandua's being held prisoner in the funnest place on earth," said Dylan.

"And the Mind Mole is still there," I said. "It's his evil lair."

CHAPTER 16

"**A**NY SIGN OF the little guy?" I said, squinting against the afternoon sun. "Sandwich crusts? Flavor-Wedge crumbs? Hamster-shaped holes in the wall?"

"Nah," said Dylan. "RaddZone still *looks* deserted." She lowered her binoculars and wiped her hands on her jeans. We had borrowed the binocs from Beefer. Despite being a little sticky, they gave a good view from the vacant lot across the street where we were hiding. The only problem was, there was nothing to see.

"I wish we could get inside and poke around a little bit," I said. "That's where Hamstersaurus Rex is."

"Did you see the little guy in your hypno-memory?" asked Dylan.

"No, but I'm sure he's there," I said. "He has to be, right?"

Too bad the funnest place on earth was locked up tight with a handwritten sign on the door that said "Closed Until Further Notice." No one entered or left. Repeated calls to what was listed as Una Raddenbach's home phone number had gone unanswered. Maple Bluffs Animal Control was still busy wrangling the other escaped weirdo critters all over town—so far my complaint had only made it down to number thirty-four in the queue. Similarly, SmilesCorp's official complaint department had refused to acknowledge our calls and messages. Finally I received a strongly worded email from SmilesCorp's lawyer's lawyer. Martha explained it was ordering me to cease and desist all communication on the matter.

Which meant saving Hammie was truly up to us now.

While Dylan and I spied on RaddZone, Martha was at her house with a stack of library books and her laptop, trying to learn more about whatever "PaleoGro" was supposed to be—and more important, guarding our canister of it against the Mind Mole's minions. We were suspicious of everyone now. When your enemy had the ability to brainwash anyone, you had no idea who to watch out for!

"Sam," said Dylan in a tone of voice that I recognized and didn't very much like. It was the same tone of voice she'd once used in kindergarten to persuade me to eat a hamburger bun full of sand. "What if we *could* get inside?"

"That would be really a bad idea," I said. "I was just blowing off steam earlier. We can't go off half-cocked. This is a recon mission. Check out RaddZone and report back."

"Well, the front door is still closed. The lights are still off. And the sign on the door hasn't changed," said Dylan. "Same as an hour ago. And an hour before that."

"Maybe if we keep watching, we'll see somebody come out or go in," I said. "Or maybe we'll discover some other clue to figuring the Mind Mole's weakness—"

"The clock is ticking," said Dylan. "Cartimandua and Hamstersaurus Rex are in real danger. Every minute we waste is a minute we won't get back."

She had a point. "Okay," I said, "we're *not* going to do what you want to do, but just for argument's sake . . . what do you want to do?"

"On my last patrol, I noticed a basement window around the back," said Dylan. "If I could pry it open, maybe I could sneak in and look around for the missing hamsters."

"Fantastic idea. One teensy little thing: *the Mind Mole is in there!*" I said. "He can drop an air hockey table on you with a thought, or worse, take control and make you his puppet. Believe me, it's no fun being mind-moled. And besides, your ankle is still broken."

"Look," said Dylan, "I can't stop thinking about what happened at school. When Cartimandua was abducted, if I hadn't let fear get the better of me, maybe things would be different right now. But instead, I ran away. Well, I hobbled away."

"It's not your fault," I said. "We saw a fern

self-destruct. Demonic lockers were slamming themselves. Anybody would have been scared."

"Doesn't matter," said Dylan. "I let you down. I let Hamstersaurus Rex down. And I want to make it right."

I sighed.

"Besides," said Dylan, "I have a foolproof plan. I won't look in his moley little eyes, and he won't be able to hypnotize me. If I hear anybody coming, I'll just do this." She closed her eyes and squinched up her whole face, tight.

"That's your foolproof plan?" I said. "This?" I squinched my own face up.

"Yep," said Dylan. "Maybe Cartimandua isn't even there anymore. But this way we'll know for sure, and we won't have to waste any more time staring at an empty building. And if she is in there, I can get her back. Hammie Rex, too!"

"Then I'll go and you stay," I said. "After all, I have full use of both my ankles. And somebody still needs to keep an eye on the front door."

Dylan frowned. "Come on, Sam. Just let me prove I can do this. I know I can."

"You've already made up your mind and you're not going to take no for an answer, are you?" I said.

"Hey, it's almost like you know me pretty well," said Dylan, putting a hand on my shoulder.

"All right," I said. "Just—just be careful in there."

"You know I will!" she said. Dylan, despite being on crutches, practically bounded off, zigzagging down the block before making a hard turn toward the window on the other side of the building. Soon she was out of sight.

I picked up the sticky binoculars and studied the front entrance to RaddZone. No one came. No one went. Still I watched, as the shadows of the cars in the parking lot slowly grew longer. The RaddZone logo on the door showed Gomer Gopher's smiling face. It felt like I'd been looking at that grotesque bucktoothed grin for an eternity. The handwritten sign still said "Closed Until Further Notice."

Left all alone, I couldn't help but worry: about Dylan, about Hamstersaurus Rex, and about Cartimandua. What did the Mind Mole even want with poor Cartimandua? She hadn't done anything. From everything I knew about her, it seemed very unlikely that she ever *would* do anything. Yet still, he had some vile mole-ish plan for her. Thinking about the twisted mutant, with his bulbous, oversized head and weird little cape, gave me a shiver. I kept remembering the words he spoke through Wilbur Weber in that horrible high-pitched voice: . . . *when we're through with you, we think you'll find that you're not so special after all!*

Just then I saw the front door to RaddZone open. I refocused the binoculars. Sure enough, it was Dylan! She shook her head and slowly walked toward me.

"Cartimandua wasn't inside," said Dylan. "Neither was Hammie Rex. The place is empty. Like Una Raddenbach unplugged the popcorn machines, turned the lights off, and left. Wherever the Mind Mole is, he's not in RaddZone anymore."

"Are you sure?" I said. "It kind of looked like he was settling in for the long term."

"I'm sure," said Dylan. "Sorry, Sam."

It was heartbreaking news. "So we're back to

square one," I said. I tossed Beefer's binoculars into my backpack. "Come on. I guess we don't need to worry about this place anymore."

The walk to Martha's house was a grim one. Neither Dylan nor I spoke.

Martha lived in a two-story house on Primrose Lane. I rang the front doorbell, and instantly the door swung open.

"Greetings, neighborhood children!" said Martha's mother, a very intense-looking woman in a bright orange turtleneck who I'd seen at school (a lot). "Unfortunately I'm afraid you've got the wrong house. Drew McCoy lives next door."

"Um, we're not here for Drew McCoy, ma'am," said Dylan.

"Ah, well, Tina Gomez actually lives on Locust Avenue around the corner," said Ms. Cherie. "It's just a hop, skip, and a jump. I can draw you a map if you like." She pulled a pen and a piece of paper out of her pocket.

"No, no. We're here to see Martha," I said.

Ms. Cherie cocked her head. "My *daughter* Martha?"

We nodded.

"What? Did she somehow miss a practice or recital or lesson or competition or performance or shift?"

We shook our heads.

"So you're not members of her competitive origami team?"

We shook our heads.

"Or fellow Antique Doll Museum interns?"

We shook her heads.

"Or Model Interplanetary Council delegates?"

"We're actually her friends," I said.

Ms. Cherie looked more confused than ever. She counted us. "But . . . there's two of you."

"We're *both* Martha's friends," said Dylan. "She has two friends."

"Well, isn't this splendid!" said Ms. Cherie, beaming. She turned to bellow back into the house. "MARTHA, DEAR, YOU HAVE TWO FRIENDS!"

"PLEASE SEND THEM UP, MOTHER," Martha bellowed back.

The inside of the Cherie residence was like one big shrine to Martha's achievements. Ribbons, awards, trophies; it was pretty much wall-to-wall accolades, and Ms. Cherie seemed determine to show us all of them.

"This is the Second-Grade Long Division Prize," she said. "Martha won it when she was in kindergarten. And this is a medal for 'Exceptional Enunciation.' Our Martha never mumbles. Oh, and of course this is an award for 'Most Awards.'"

"Wow," I said, feigning interest in the Martha Hall of Fame. "And to think she's only twelve. What are you going to do with all the trophies she *hasn't* won yet?"

Ms. Cherie thought about this. "We'll probably need a bigger house," she said matter-of-factly.

Dylan nudged me with her elbow. "None of these are for sports," she whispered, and she gave a contemptuous shrug.

"And this is Martha's room," said Ms. Cherie. She knocked. "Martha, your, ahem, *friends* are here."

"Password, please," said Martha from inside. We didn't know whether or not a password would thwart a mind-controlled minion of the Mind Mole, but we figured it couldn't hurt.

"*Mesocricetus*," I said.

Ms. Cherie squinted at me.

"It's the scientific genus for hamsters or something," I said, with a shrug.

"You kids and your hamsters!" said Ms. Cherie. "From what Martha tells me, they're all the rage these days."

"Sure. I guess," I said.

Martha's door opened, and Dylan and I stepped inside. As one might expect, it was tidy and full of books (all nonfiction). A Victorian dollhouse stood in the corner, and there were a few dozen dolls on a display shelf nearby. Clearly none of them had ever been played with.

"Hey, kind of like a miniature Antique Doll Museum," said Dylan, nodding toward the doll shelf.

"Actually, my own personal collection is highly contemporary," said Martha. "No dolls here older than six months."

"Well, I tried to make conversation," said Dylan with a shrug as she plopped down on Martha's bed.

"RaddZone is empty," I said. "No Mind Mole. No Cartimandua. No Hammie."

"Drat and fiddlefluffs!" said Martha. "Pardon my language."

"Any luck figuring out what PaleoGro is?" I said.

Martha shook her head. "There's no mention of it in any of my chemistry or biology books, and I haven't found anything online yet. SmilesCorp used it in trace amounts in a couple of their health products, but they never actually said what it does."

"Well, good luck getting anything out of those guys," said Dylan. "They'll probably deny there's actually a company called SmilesCorp."

"Bad news after bad news," I said. "So, we're stuck. What are we supposed to do now?"

"We could put these custom patches on our sleeves," said Martha. She held up a cloth diamond that said "A Hamster Monitor Always Gets Her Hamster" on it.

"They're iron-ons," she added.

"Wait a second," said Dylan, leaping to her feet. "I think I *finally* remembered where I heard of PaleoGro somewhere before. Can I see the label?"

Martha nodded and went toward the dollhouse in the corner. It was actually an electronic safe.

"Normally I only keep my Perfect Attendance pins in here," said Martha as she punched a four-digit code into an electronic keypad hidden underneath the doormat. I heard the click of a bolt sliding. Martha opened the hinged roof of the house and pulled out the canister. She handed it to Dylan.

"Guys, wait right here," said Dylan. "I'll be back in an hour." She started toward the door.

"Hang on," I said.

Dylan paused.

"You forgot your crutches." I pointed to them, leaning against the wall.

"So I did," said Dylan with a chuckle. "So I did." As she turned to get them, I snatched the Paleo-Gro out of her hands.

"Sam, what are you doing?" screeched Dylan.

"Don't let her have this!" I yelled as I tossed the canister to Martha.

"Aaaagh!" shrieked Martha as Dylan tackled her, jostling several contemporary dolls right off the shelf.

"Give it to us!" hissed Dylan, clawing for the PaleoGro.

"Sam, help!" screamed Martha as she flicked the PaleoGro back in my general direction. Instead of landing in my outstretched palms, it ricocheted off a Debbie Future doll, shattering her head. I spun and bobbled the canister once, twice, but finally got both hands on it.

"Hand over the PaleoGro!" squealed Dylan in a grating, high-pitched voice. "We require it!"

"Nope," I said, holding the PaleoGro as high up as I could. "Nuh-uh. No way."

In an instant, Dylan was up and running toward me.

"Dylan, stop!" I said.

She was building up speed.

"Even though you've been hypnotized, I know you're still in there!" I cried. "I want to speak to my best friend since preschool. Dylan D'Amato, are you—"

Dylan lowered her head like a battering ram and butted me in the stomach, hard, knocking the wind out of my lungs. I wheezed and dropped the PaleoGro, which bounced under Martha's bed.

"Ours! Ours! Ours!" screeched Dylan as she dove under the bed. Somehow I grabbed her good ankle and managed to drag her back out.

A second later, Martha landed on Dylan's back. "This is a Hamster Monitor arrest!" she screamed as she tried to hold Dylan down. "You have the right to remain—OWWW!"

Dylan chomped down on Martha's elbow. "Get off of us!" screeched Dylan as she squirmed and bucked while Martha held on for dear life. Their jostling tipped the doll shelf over.

"Sam, the canister!" screamed Martha.

I dove under the bed and groped around until I found the PaleoGro. Then I scrambled back across the broken doll shrapnel now carpeting the floor to the other side of the room. I plunked the PaleoGro into Martha's dollhouse safe and slammed the roof closed. The safe locked itself with a beep.

"There, now you can't get it!" I yelled to Dylan. "You hear me, Mind Mole? You're out of luck, you creep!"

Dylan stopped struggling. She turned to stare at me with pure malice in her eyes. "You refuse to relinquish the PaleoGro, so we'll make it a trade: the canister for Cartimandua's life. Tomorrow at noon. You know where to find us. And bring the 'Hamster Hero of Horace Hotwater' with you! He shall bear witness!"

Dylan let out an evil squealing cackle; then she convulsed violently for a few seconds and was perfectly still. Martha and I looked at each other, panting.

"Martha, is she . . . ?"

Martha checked Dylan's pulse.

"Gaaaaaaaah!" screamed Dylan, sitting bolt upright. She blinked and looked around the room. "Why are we all covered in doll parts?"

There was a knock on the door. "Martha, sweetie," called Ms. Cherie, "is everything okay in there with your non-extracurricular friends?"

"Yes, Mother!" cried Martha, rubbing the bite marks on her elbow. "Please disregard the noises you heard. We're just engaging in horseplay. We are children, after all."

It took a good half hour to convince Dylan she was the latest victim of the Mind Mole. After we finally did, she was furious with herself.

"I can't believe I was so stupid," said Dylan, shaking her head. "Ugh. I'm totally useless."

"Not *totally* useless," said Martha.

"Martha!" I said, glaring at her.

"I mean, thanks to Dylan's mista—er, *investigation*," said Martha, "at least we now know that the Mind Mole is definitely inside RaddZone. And that he doesn't have Hamstersaurus Rex captive."

"You're right!" I said. "Otherwise he wouldn't have told us to bring him!" I was momentarily filled with hope. But just as quickly, my spirits fell. "Except we have less than a day to deliver the PaleoGro with the little guy in tow, or Cartimandua gets it. How are we possibly going to find Hamstersaurus Rex?"

By the looks on Martha's and Dylan's faces, they didn't have an answer.

BRRRRRRING! Martha's phone startled us all. Martha hesitated, then answered it.

"Cherie residence, Martha Madeline Cherie speaking," she said. "Oh, uh-huh. No, I don't have a crush on anyone right now. Yes, I'm positive. Oh? Oh, really? Excelsior!" Martha hung up.

"That was Beefer," she said. "He found Hamstersaurus Rex."

CHAPTER 17

I **WENT TO THE** address Beefer had given me—633 West Ramblewood Street—but Beefer wasn't there. So I stood in the leafy courtyard of an apartment building called The Ramblewood Arms and waited.

"Pssst!"

I turned around and saw nothing. Just two blue mailboxes on the corner beside a bush. Wait, why were there two? A hand poked out of the one on the left and beckoned me.

"Beefer, are you dressed as a mailbox?" I said.

"Yup," said Beefer. "Pretty sweet, huh? There was a make-your-own-mailbox-costume tutorial in the June issue of *Pustule*, the premier special effects magazine for tweens. This baby is professional quality. Just like you might see in a big-budget Hollywood movie!"

"Do a lot of Hollywood movies need mailbox costumes?" I asked.

"Did you ever see *The Night the Mailboxes Came to Life and Bit People's Hands and Feet?*"

"Uh, nope," I said.

"Zero respect for the arts," muttered Beefer. "You bring my binoculars?"

I pulled them out of my backpack.

"Check the third floor, second window from the right," he said. "And don't get your eye grease all over them!"

"Eye grease?!" I said. "These binoculars already feel like the floor of a movie theater! What do you clean them with, maple syrup?"

"Now isn't the time for insults, dummy," said Beefer. "Just look!"

I scanned the third floor until I got to the

second window from the right. In its corner I noticed a small wire cage. Inside it, jogging away in a hamster wheel, was my favorite mutant in the world!

"It's Hamstersaurus Rex!" I cried.

"Duh, and also, you're welcome," said Beefer. "Using my amazing ninja skills, I got the drop on Purple Hair and followed her back here. This is where she lives. Apartment 3F. Sandoval."

"Should I buzz?" I said.

"No way, are you crazy?" said Beefer. "She's evil!"

"Fine. You're right," I said. "So what should we do?"

"Don't worry. As always, yours truly has a plan," said Beefer. "We're going to need grappling hooks and a couple dozen smoke bombs. You're a nerd; do you think you can program a computer virus that would make all the elevators in an apartment building go crazy?"

"Definitely not," I said.

"Why are you talking to a mailbox?" came a voice from behind me.

I whipped around to see the purple-haired girl

staring at me. She had chunky oversized head-phones on and a messenger bag slung over her shoulder.

"Don't tell her!" hissed Beefer.

"I'll answer your question if you tell me why you kidnapped my hamster," I said.

"Easy, guy. Don't have a hamst-eurism," said Purple Hair. "I didn't *kidnap* him. I found him wandering around depressed. To answer your second question, your friend drilled me in the face with a golf disc. Oh, and that other guy tried to ninja me until I kicked him."

"Wasn't a fair fight," said Beefer. "I could crush you if I wanted to!"

"Okay, is he *inside* that mailbox?" said Purple Hair.

"Please don't tell her!" squealed Beefer.

"Who do you work for?" I said. "SmilesCorp?"

"No way!" she cried. "Well, sort of. But not *exactly*."

"What kind of an answer is that?" cried Beefer.

"Let me explain," she said.

"Just tell me if you're under the hypnotic power

of an evil telepathic mole or not!" I cried.

Her eyes widened. "Do you mean Specimen #4449?"

"Um. Maybe?" I said.

"No, I'm not, Sam. But I think you better come inside," she said. "Bring your mailbox, too." She started to walk toward the door of the Ramble-wood Arms.

"Who are you?" I said.

"My name's Serena Sandoval," said the purple-haired girl.

She lived in a two-bedroom apartment with her dad, who wasn't home from work yet.

"You guys want anything?" said Serena as she looked in the fridge. "We have water and . . . pickles."

"Hmm. I'll take some pickle water," said Beefer. "Best of both worlds."

Serena and I both gagged.

"What?" said Beefer. "It's full of essential pickle nutrients! Eight tall glasses of pickle water a day is how I keep this physique."

Serena shook her head and poured some of the

greenish water from the pickle jar into a plastic cup for Beefer.

"Anything for you, Sam?" she said.

"Just my stolen hamster slash best friend," I said.

"Wow, guilt trip much?" said Serena. "Fine. This way."

Her room was nearly as messy as Beefer's. The walls were covered with posters for bands I'd never heard of (Adversity Dog, Warlock Toddler, Mary and the Feet). She saw me looking at them.

"You've probably never heard of these bands," she said.

"I've heard of, uh, *some* of them," I lied.

On her cluttered desk was the hamster cage I'd seen from outside, with Hamstersaurus Rex still racing in the wheel. He turned and spotted me. Then the little guy let out a mighty roar. To the untrained ear—and Serena's neighbors—it probably sounded terrifying. But I knew the little guy was happy to see me. I almost roared myself.

"Okay, Spikehead," said Serena. "Time to go back to your real owner."

"*Spikehead?!*" I said. "His name is Hamster-saurus Rex!"

"Hamstersaurus Rex," said Serena, pondering it. "That's kinda . . . meh."

"I know!" said Beefer. "Some people wanted to call him 'Martha Jr.' but nobody even cared what they thought."

Serena opened the cage and took the little guy out. As she did, he cooed and nuzzled her hand. I felt a momentary pang of something.

"Aw, man, your gerbil totally loves her," said Beefer, prodding me with his elbow. "Maybe more than he loves you? Wow, that's got to hurt. Does it hurt? It's *got* to!"

"Just drink your pickle water, man," I said.

"Gladly," said Beefer. And he loudly savored a big slurp.

It was true, though. Hamstersaurus Rex seemed to like Serena, maybe more than anyone (except me!). In fact, he didn't seem depressed at all anymore. And it was clear that she really liked him, too. She grinned and her eyes twinkled as she tickled his scaly belly. I felt like I'd seen her eyes somewhere before, I just couldn't put my finger on where.

Serena handed Hamstersaurus Rex over to me. The little guy jumped up and down and slobbered all over my face, neck, shoulders, and legs. Some got on my shoes, too.

"Good to have you back, Hammie," I said, scratching him on the tip of his dino-tail. He gurgled.

"For what it's worth, I think Spikehead really missed you," said Serena.

"So why *have* you been following us?" I asked.

"Yeah," said Beefer, wiping a pickle-water moustache off his lips with the back of his sleeve. "And more important, how do we know you're not a werewolf?"

"Dunno." Serena shrugged. "I'm a vegetarian?"

"Ugh," said Beefer, crossing his arms. "Worse than a werewolf."

"Anyway," said Serena. "I figured out it was you two who broke into SmilesCorp, and then I figured out you helped stop that giant squirrel . . . and, I dunno."

"How did you possibly figure all that out?" I said. "SmilesCorp made sure there was no news coverage of either one of those things."

"I know. Too bad I'm super awesome at figuring stuff out," said Serena. "Plus I had an in at Smiles-Corp. My great-aunt Sue used to work there."

Alarm bells went off in my head. "That's where I recognize you from!" I cried. "You look just like the portrait of Sue Sandoval that we saw inside SmilesCorp! She was your great-aunt? Now I don't know if you're evil or not again!" I hugged Hammie Rex close to me.

"I'm not!" said Serena. "You're getting thrown by the purple hair!"

"But Sue Sandoval used to be head of the SmilesCorp Genetic Research and Development Lab, where they made Squirrel Kong and a bunch of other freaky mutant animals!" I said.

"They turned Michael Perkins into a boakeet," said Beefer.

"No idea what that means, guy," said Serena. "But you're right, my great-aunt *was* lab chief until last year. And she did help make those weird animals! But by the end she really regretted it."

"The end?" I said.

"She passed away a few months ago," said Serena. "We were pretty tight."

"I'm—I'm sorry to hear that," I said.

Serena shrugged. "Luckily she left behind boxes and boxes of papers and journals. I started reading through her stuff, and I realized that she eventually regretted a lot of her choices. She thought what SmilesCorp was doing was wrong, and she worried that the mutants she had helped make could be really dangerous. Especially if they ever escaped from SmilesCorp."

"Which they totally have," I said.

"Bingo," said Serena. "I figured that out from all the local chatter I read on truthblasters.com."

"See! It is a reputable journalistic source!" cried Beefer.

"Nah, it's basically full of cranks," said Serena. "Anyway, I wanted to learn more. So I used the ol' family connection to get an externship at SmilesCorp."

"So you *do* work for them!" I said.

"Not really. I'm embedded," said Serena. "I'm, like, deep, deep undercover. On alternating Wednesday afternoons."

"Undercover?" I said.

"See, what I actually am is a journalist," said Serena. "Well, I want to be one. I'm going to start a blog one day. When the time is right. Anyway, I'm working on my first story, and it's going to blow the lid off SmilesCorp, and this bad boy gets me in the door." She showed me a SmilesCorp ID card that looked just like my mom's. "While I'm fetching coffee for people and pretending I care about what bagels we should have in the conference room, I can poke around and learn things they don't want me to learn."

"But that *still* doesn't explain why you followed us," I said.

"Right. Okay, so I was trying to make sure we were on the same side," said Serena. "I think we are. And this is going to sound awkward, but I

SPECIMEN #3010

figured we could, you know, team up or whatever." She stared at the floor like she was embarrassed.

"Fat chance," said Beefer. "We don't work with vegetarians! Right, Sam?"

"Ignore him," I said. "What exactly did you have in mind?"

"For starters: here are my great-aunt's notes on all SmilesCorp's mutant creatures. I think they might help," said Serena. She hefted an overflowing manila folder out of her messenger bag and slapped it down on her desk with a thunk. As she paged through it, I could see that each sheet had a photo of a strange mutant animal attached. I recognized scaly mice, the Grizzly Hare, and a chicken that looked like a turtle. Serena found the pages she was looking for and handed them to me. "Feast your eyes on this handsome devil," she said.

The document was titled "Specimen #4449—*Scalopus psionicus*." It was columns

SPECIMEN #5399673

SPECIMEN #52

of numbers and incomprehensible text, a whole lot of scientific jargon I didn't understand. I certainly recognized the photo stapled to the corner, though. It was a blurry image of an evil-looking mole with a grotesquely oversized head.

"The Mind Mole," I said with a shudder. "But I don't really get what the file, um, *means*."

"Honestly, he's not that smart," said Beefer to Serena.

"Yeah, I've read it roughly one bazillion times myself and I still don't understand most of it," said Serena. "But the gist of it is, Specimen #4449 is this genetically engineered mole. His brain size was increased five thousand percent, granting him superior intelligence, mind control, and telekinesis. My great-aunt was worried. She thought he

SPECIMEN #4449

was probably the most dangerous mutant Smiles-Corp ever created."

"After the past week, I'd say that checks out," I said. "He nearly dropped a plaster sea turtle on me *with his mind*."

"Far out," said Serena.

"So does Specimen #4449 have any weaknesses?" I asked.

"You mean like a food allergy or something?" said Serena. She shrugged. "Like I said, man, I don't understand all the science-speak myself."

"Good thing I know someone who does," I said.

". . . Are you talking about me?" whispered Beefer.

"No, I *obviously* mean Martha," I said with a sigh. "All right, you've got a deal, Serena. It's a good old-fashioned team-up."

I held out my hand and Serena shook it. Hamstersaurus Rex let out an eager snarl. The little guy was back, and he was itching for action.

"Serena, he was super bummed out when you found him," I said. "What changed his mood?"

"I dunno. I just showed him a bunch of pictures

and some old home movies of my great-aunt Sue," said Serena. "She really loved the little guy. And I can understand why." She made a weird face and crossed her eyes at Hammie and he grunted happily.

"Wait. Dr. Sue Sandoval knew Hamstersaurus Rex?" I said, shocked.

"Duh," said Serena. "She was the one who created him."

CHAPTER 18

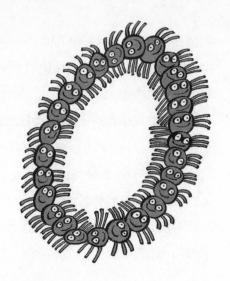

BACK AT MARTHA'S house, Ms. Cherie was pleasantly surprised that her daughter apparently now had *four* friends.

"Hmm. I wonder if Martha could win some sort of medal for her total friend count," said Ms. Cherie as she led us up to Martha's room. Dylan was already waiting inside.

Before I could say anything, Beefer elbowed past me. "Salutatorians, Martha," he said, offering an awkward bow. "Sorry we meet again under such indigestible circumstances. But I hope this small token of my amalgamation will brighten your day, m'lady." He held out a necklace that looked like it was made of interlocking metal spiders. "I got it out of a claw machine," he added.

"Thank you, Kiefer," said Martha, taking the necklace. "Perhaps I can wear this on August twenty-third, which is National Brown Recluse Awareness Day."

"Or any time!" said Beefer. "Formal, unformal, Halloween, Earth Day. You can wear a spider necklace whenever you want!"

"Hmm," said Martha, dropping the necklace into a drawer.

"Guys, look who's back," I said. I took Hamstersaurus Rex out of my pocket and put him on the floor. Dylan and Martha cheered. The little guy gave a triumphant stomp that rattled the windows.

"Martha?" called Ms. Cherie from downstairs.

"Horseplay, Mother!" screamed Martha.

"Also, I want you to meet Serena Sandoval," I said. "She's totally not evil!"

"Vegetarian, though," said Beefer.

"Hi," said Serena, looking around. "Your room is really . . . organized." She picked up a label maker.

"Please don't move that," said Martha, putting

it back where Serena had gotten it.

"Sorry I hit you in the face with a golf disc," said Dylan. "Somebody add it to the long list of mistakes I've made."

"No hard feelings," said Serena. "It made a cool welt that kinda looks like Japan." She showed everyone. It *was* pretty cool.

"Martha, Serena has something else you need to see, too," I said. "Besides the Japan welt."

"Oh yeah," said Serena. She handed over the manila folder, opened to the Mind Mole's file.

Martha scanned it. "Wow," she said. "Where did you get this?"

Serena gave Martha and Dylan the whole backstory of her great-aunt's work at SmilesCorp.

"So Sue Sandoval somehow *created* Hamster-saurus Rex?" said Martha.

"Crazy, right?" I said. "I guess he's technically an escaped SmilesCorp mutant, too!"

"Yeah, Spikehead's file is in there if you want to take a look," said Serena.

"Spikehead?" said Martha.

"No time. We need to focus on the Mind Mole,"

I said. "At this point we've got less than a day to come up with a plan to save Cartimandua and end that little caped creep's reign of terror."

Hamstersaurus Rex gave an angry snort. I could tell he hated the thought of Cartimandua being held captive.

"Right," said Martha. "I'll study Specimen #4999's file. Try to determine whether there's something in it we can use against the Mind Mole."

"Awesome," I said.

"So RaddZone is where he's keeping Carburetor?" said Serena.

"*Cartimandua*," said Martha.

"If you say so," said Serena. "Anyway, maybe I can poke around a bit and find the blueprints to the building. Could give us the edge?"

"Great," I said.

"And I can make custom ninja masks for everyone!" said Beefer. "I need a new one 'cause mine ripped."

"Huh. Okay, fine. I guess," I said. "Dylan?"

Dylan gave a shrug. "Dunno. I should probably sit this one out."

We all stared at her. Even Hamstersaurus Rex.

"But you're a Hamster Monitor," said Martha. "You took the oath."

"I know, I know," said Dylan. "But I've done nothing but make the wrong choice at every single turn lately. Yeah, I'm not *actually* cursed by a vengeful pioneer ghost, but the alternative is even worse. Besides, I've got a broken ankle."

"But we need you," I said. "Right, guys?"

Martha and Beefer nodded.

"I just met her, but sure," said Serena. "What was that about a pioneer ghost?"

"Don't worry about it," I said.

"Okay, okay," said Dylan glumly. "I guess I could, uh, try to figure out what PaleoGro is. I probably won't be able to."

"Fantastic," I said. "Hammie and I will go back to Maple Bluffs Animal Control. We can try one last time to get them to take the case."

"Tomorrow is Saturday, which means unfortunately we don't have school," said Martha. "Let's reconvene here to strategize at nine a.m. sharp."

"See you then!" I said. I grabbed Hamstersaurus Rex and ran for the door.

Half an hour later, I was standing in the lobby of Maple Bluffs Animal Control, pleading with Agent Gould.

"Good news: your complaint is now number fifteen in the queue," said Agent Gould. "We're probably going to get to it next week."

"Next week?" I said. "But tomorrow, the evil mole that I reported earlier—who's called the Mind Mole, by the way, on account of his dangerous mental powers—is going to kill our new class hamster, Cartimandua!"

Agent Gould cocked her head. "Sorry, kid, but there are certain protocols we have to follow. We've got to catch that chicken that looks like a turtle first. Off the record, that case has *really* been throwing us for a loop. We keep arresting innocent chickens."

"It doesn't even look like a chicken!" I cried. "Can you please, please, please, please, please just send someone to RaddZone to check it out? It's an emergency!"

Agent Gould sighed. She drummed her fingers on the table. She looked at the queue, then at the clock. She sighed again. "All right, kid, let me radio McKay."

"Yes!" I cried, and pumped my fist. I felt Hammie Rex squirm for joy in my pocket.

Agent Gould got on the office's dispatch radio. "Verminator Two, this is Verminator One, do you copy? Over."

The radio crackled. "Verminator One, this is Verminator Two. Go ahead. Over."

"Verminator Two, we've got reports of a telepathic mole infestation at RaddZone—that's the big arcade and mini-golf place out at the West Oaks Shopping Center beside the Coat Barn. Over."

"Home of the RaddSpudd? Over."

"That's the place. Over."

"I'm on it!" said Agent McKay. In the background I heard tires squeal. "Over and out." The radio crackled and was silent.

I waited there for ten minutes or so,

forced to make awkward small talk with Agent Gould. She had her eye on a new propane grill. But it was probably too expensive. But she still might buy it. I looked at the clock myself. Suddenly the radio crackled again.

"Verminator One, this is Verminator Two. Come in, Verminator One? Over."

"I copy you, Verminator Two," said Agent Gould. "What's the status on that telepathic mole dealie? Over."

"Yep, that's a negatory, Verminator One," said McKay. "RaddZone was totally deserted. No moles, repeat no moles, telepathic or otherwise. Over."

"But I know the Mind Mole is there!" I cried. "I know he is!"

Agent Gould frowned. "You absolutely sure, Verminator Two? Over."

"Absolutely. But we have received reports of a dangerous mutant hamster in your area; answers to the name of Hamstersaurus Rex. Could be rabid. Neutralize and apprehend with extreme prejudice!"

"What?" I said, backing away and reflexively

clutching at Hammie, hidden in my pocket. "That's not— Oh no! Listen to me; Agent McKay has been mind-moled!"

Agent Gould stood up from her desk. "Kid, do you know anything about what my partner is talking about? Have you seen a dangerous mutant rabid hamster?"

"No," I said. "Gotta go."

"Wait!"

But I was already out the door. I could hear the sound of evil, high-pitched laughter crackling over the dispatch radio behind me.

CHAPTER 19

THE NEXT MORNING, I stood on Martha Cherie's porch at 8:59 a.m. Everyone else had gotten there on time, too: Dylan, Serena, and even Beefer. I rang the doorbell.

Martha answered the door, grinning. "Friends! I stayed up half the night studying Specimen #4449's file," she said as she led us up to her room, "and I found the Mind Mole's fatal weakness!"

"What is it?" said Dylan.

"Physically, he's pathetic," said Martha. "All his increased brainpower stunted his muscular development."

"Hmm," said Beefer. "So he's sort of like the Sam of the animal kingdom."

"Exactly," said Martha.

"Hey!" I said.

"The Mind Mole couldn't claw his way out of a wet paper bag," said Martha. "And one good bump on his soft, swollen head would probably knock him out cold."

"Rad," said Serena. "Except between the telekinesis and the mind control, how exactly is somebody supposed to get close enough to do that?"

"I have no idea," said Martha, still beaming.

"Great," I said. "So he *has* a weakness, we just can't exploit it."

"Correct," said Martha. "Would anyone like a sugar-free, flour-free beet muffin?"

She held up a tray of them. Everyone passed.

"Well, at least I was able to find the blueprints for the West Oaks Shopping Center on the town archives website. Investigative reporting!" said Serena as she pulled a bunch of crumpled print-outs from her messenger bag. "Did you guys know there's this window in the basement around back of RaddZone that we could use to—"

"We know," I said. "And the Mind Mole does, too. It's not a secret anymore."

"Thanks to me," said Dylan with a sigh. "Oh, and I didn't actually figure out what PaleoGro is, by the way. Sorry."

"Wow," said Beefer. "Looks like I'm the only one who promised and delivered."

"Oh, so you made the custom ninja masks for all of us?" I said. "Fantastic, Beefer. Thank you sooooo much."

Beefer frowned and turned to the group. "So rude. Now do you all see what I have to put up with?"

They nodded.

"Sorry," I said. "Thanks for chipping in, I guess." I plopped down on Martha's bed. "I'm just frustrated because at this rate, there's no way we'll be able to stop the Mind Mole and save Cartimandua."

Hamstersaurus Rex gave a snarl. Serena fed him a sardine. I didn't know he liked sardines.

"Maybe we could all blindfold ourselves," I said. "His mind-control power requires direct eye contact. If we don't look into the Mind Mole's eyes, he can't hypnotize us."

"Um, if we're all blindfolded, how are we even going to move around and stuff, much less save Carta-Magna?" said Serena.

"Her name is Cartimandua," snapped Martha. "It's really not that hard."

"Serena's right," said Dylan. "I already tried to keep my eyes closed. Didn't exactly work out for me, now did it? Everybody who has crossed paths with the Mind Mole has ended up getting hypnotized: Gordon Renfro, Wilbur, Jared, Sam, me, and now Agent McKay. No one was able to resist."

"Hang on! That's not true!" I cried as I suddenly remembered. "There *was* someone who looked at him and didn't get hypnotized!" I leaped to my feet. "Gotta go! Everybody keep working on an awesome, foolproof master plan, but there's one more person I need to talk to. I'll be back in an hour. I've got a hunch!" I dashed for the door.

* * *

Hamstersaurus Rex and I stood on the porch of an old house with flaking paint and a weedy, overgrown yard. Forget school, I thought, *this* was a place the ghost of Horace Hotwater ought to haunt. Hammie Rex shot me a quizzical look, as if to ask why we were here.

"This is where Old Man Ohlman lives," I said. "You know, the tinfoil hat guy who complained to Agent Gould about seeing that creepy mole. He must have been talking about the Mind Mole!"

I rapped on the door. There was no answer.

"Hello, Old Ma— I mean, *Mister* Ohlman?" I yelled. "Are you home, sir?"

Inside, I heard someone stirring. I knocked again. At last the inner door swung open. Old Man Ohlman, as always wearing his tinfoil hat, glared at me from inside the screen. "I told the other fellow from the telephone company that I'm actually quite fond of bees!" he yelled. "I thought that would be the end of it! But here you are, all set to ruin my Tuesday!"

"What? No. It's Saturday."

"You don't think a Tuesday can be ruined on a

Saturday?" said Old Man Ohlman. "That shows a dearth of imagination!"

"Look, I'm not from the telephone company," I said. "I'm a sixth grader."

He squinted at me. "So did you hit a baseball into my backyard, then?" said Old Man Ohlman. "Sorry, sonny, that baseball is mine now! I got hundreds of 'em. Boy, if you saw my collection you'd cry. Hee hee."

"That's not what I'm here about either. I want to ask you about a mole!"

"You mean the one on my elbow?" he said. "I happen to like the way it looks, and that's all I care to say on that matter!" He rolled his sleeve down so I couldn't see the mole on his elbow.

"No, no," I said. "Like a mole that digs in the ground and eats bugs and stuff."

"Are you funning at my expense, young fella?" he said. "For shame! I'm a veteran of the Franco-Prussian War. I have half a mind to tell you to get gone. You're scarin' away all my best bees!"

I looked around. "I don't see any bees."

"Aw, nuts! Then you already done scared 'em!"

He shook his head mournfully and started to shut the door.

"Sir, please just hear me out," I said. "I was there when you made your complaint."

"I make complaints all day, every day, to anyone who will listen," said Old Man Ohlman. "You're going to have to be more specific."

"At Maple Bluffs Animal Control, you said you saw a mole that looked at you 'real mean.'"

Old Man Ohlman pondered this. "Indeed I did. Had a head like a cantaloupe. Stared at me like he was tryin' to drill a hole through me with them little eyes. What of it?"

"I want to know what happened then," I said. "Did the mole . . . command you to do things?"

"*Command me?!* What are you, nuts, kid? It was a mole!" said Old Man Ohlman. "What happened then was that I yelled at it to get off my lawn and it did. And then I yelled at some pinecones to get off my lawn and they just sat there. Incredibly rude!"

"Just like I thought," I cried. "You're immune to the Mind Mole's powers!"

"Young man, I got to tell you, you are truly eccentric," said Old Man Ohlman. "And that's coming from *me!*"

"Mr. Ohlman, you've got to help me," I said. "My class hamster is in grave danger and you're the only one in the world who can save her!"

A faraway look came over Old Man Ohlman as he stared out toward the horizon. "Is this finally my chance?" he said, almost to himself. "To right wrongs? Stick up for the powerless and realize my true potential? After a long and cranky life of cantankerous cootery, is now the moment when I, Foster Olroyd Ohlman VII, become . . . *a true hero?*" He licked his gums. "Nah. I gotta polish my Baby President figurines. Later, kid!"

"What?" I cried.

Hamstersaurus Rex popped out of my pocket and roared at his terrible attitude.

"Ha!" said Old Man Ohlman. "You think I never been roared at by a hamster before? Go on, now! Get gone! You'll attract bees!"

And with that, he slammed the front door in my face.

It was a long, sad walk back to Martha's house. Our only hope for stopping the Mind Mole had decided to polish his Baby President figurines instead. I privately hoped he broke one.

"Don't worry, dude," I said to Hamstersaurus Rex. "We'll think of something."

Back in Martha's room, everyone was hard at work. Beefer and Serena were arguing over the RaddZone blueprints. Serena was arranging the few unbroken Debbie Future dolls for tactical placement while Beefer overexplained to her how to use his set of bulky walkie-talkies. Martha was studying Sue Sandoval's notes and cross-referencing with a stack of science textbooks. Dylan alone sat in the corner, lost in thought.

"How'd that hunch pan out?" she asked.

"Wasted effort," I said as I flopped down on the floor. Hammie Rex licked my face. "The one person in the whole world who seems to be immune to the Mind Mole's power—"

"Power! That's it!" cried Dylan. "I just remembered where I've seen PaleoGro before!"

We all turned to stare at her. Even Hamstersaurus Rex.

"A little while back," said Dylan, "I was alone in Coach Weekes's office. He was in the boys' locker room, and I was waiting for him to finish dying his moustache—"

"*He dyes it?!*" cried Martha.

"Oh yeah," said Dylan. "That thing is as white as the driven snow."

"Who's Coach Weekes?" said Serena.

"Tell you later. It's a whole thing," I said. "Dylan, please continue."

"Well, I didn't have anything else to do, so I started looking at the stuff on his shelves. I got to reading labels of his health supplements. Along with ten percent Biceptrex, thirteen percent reconstituted bison whey, seventy-six percent ground pill bug meal, Dinoblast Powerpacker is exactly one percent PaleoGro."

"DinoBlast Powerpacker?" I said. "That's the junk that Hamstersaurus Rex ate that turned him half dinosaur!"

"Oh no," said Martha. "This is bad. This is really, really bad."

"What?" I said.

"Sam, while you were gone, I took a look at the file Dr. Sandoval kept on Hamstersaurus Rex," said Martha. "Hammie has genetic receptors coded into his DNA that were designed to activate when exposed to a mystery chemical. In the file, the name of the chemical is redacted."

"Um," said Beefer, "for Sam's benefit, what does reda—"

"Marked out," said Martha. "But now I *know* that the mystery chemical must be PaleoGro."

"So?" I said.

"So, Specimen #4449 has the same genetic receptors," said Martha. "That's why he wants the stuff."

It slowly dawned on me what she was saying.

"The Mind Mole is going to use the PaleoGro to eliminate his one weakness," said Martha. "He's going to give himself dinosaur powers. Just like Hamstersaurus Rex."

"Then we can't hand it over," said Serena. "With dino-strength on top of his freaky mental powers, he'll be . . ."

"Unstoppable," I said. "But what choice do we have? Cartimandua's life is on the line and time is almost up. We have to do it."

"Well," said Serena. "The good news is that I think I *may* have found another way in."

CHAPTER 20

AT 11:37 A.M., Martha, Beefer, Serena, Dylan, Hammie Rex, and I entered the Coat Barn at the West Oaks Shopping Center. We weren't there for the "Best of the Vest: Mega Sale on Tweed Vests." In fact, we had no intention of buying anything at all. We were on a mission.

We huddled around a circular rack of factory-irregular parkas in a deserted corner of the massive store. No one was watching. I gave a nod. We ducked inside the rack.

"Okay. It should be just inside the dressing rooms to the left," said Serena. "An old service entrance that connects Coat Barn to RaddZone next door."

"Nice work, Serena," I said.

"Thanks, guy," said Serena. "Hopefully we don't all die."

"I feel like going through the door is maybe, probably, definitely against the rules," said Martha. "What if somebody calls the security guard we all end up in prison?"

"An innocent hamster's life is on the line," I said. "What does that patch on your jacket say?"

"Spelling Bee District Champion," said Martha.

"Other arm," I said.

She looked. "A Hamster Monitor Always Gets Her Hamster." Martha gave a resolute nod.

"Besides," I said, "the Mind Mole must be stopped, and no one else is going to do it for us. He's an evil little creep with a chip on his shoulder that's even bigger than his melon head. With his powers, he can control anyone. So far it's been limited to our little town. But think of all the damage he could do if he put his twisted mind to it."

Hammie Rex seconded this with a loud growl. I shushed him and hoped we hadn't spooked any customers who might be shopping for irregular parkas. Luckily it was a very slow Saturday for Coat Barn.

"All right," I said. "The plan requires one of us to hang back."

"I'll do it," said Dylan.

"You sure?" I said.

"If I go with you guys, I'll just mess up again," said Dylan. "Safer to have me here, where I can't blow it too bad."

"Okay, if that's what you want," I said. "Beefer?"

"Try not to get your ear grease all over this," said Beefer as he handed her one of his walkie-talkies.

"You'll need these, too," I said. I reached into my backpack and handed her my old laptop and the blueprints that Serena had printed out. "The clock is ticking. Everybody ready?"

Martha nodded and touched her arm patch. Dylan gave me a wry thumbs-up. Serena shot me a peace sign. Hamstersaurus Rex snarled, ready for action.

"Wait!" cried Beefer. He started to rummage around in his duffel bag.

"C'mon, Beefer," I said. "We really don't have time to waste."

"This is important!" he said as he pulled out a piece of purple cloth and handed it to Serena. She unfolded it. It was a ninja mask.

"You made this?" said Serena.

"Yep," said Beefer. "It's purple, on account of your hair. I figured purple was probably your favorite color."

"It's not, but thanks," said Serena. "This is weirdly . . . thoughtful." She put her mask on.

"Dylan, for you," said Beefer. He handed her a ninja mask upon which he had monogrammed the word "DISCWIPERS."

"Discwipers?" said Dylan.

"It's your disc golf team!" cried Beefer.

"Oh, right," said Dylan. "Yep, that's us: the Horace Hotwater Disc*wipers*." She put her mask on. "Thanks, Beef."

"And a most regurgitated mask for you, m'lady," said Beefer. He pulled out a grayish speckled ninja mask with an odd spiral horn coming out of it.

Martha's eyes lit up. "It's a narwhal," said

Martha. "That happens to be my favorite northern-latitudes sea mammal!"

"I know," said Beefer. "I've always known."

Martha hugged him. Beefer yanked on his own mask. "And mine's covered in music notes on account of my interest in Renaissance music. Well, that's pretty much everybody. Let's go."

"Hey," I said. "What about me?"

"Oh yeah," said Beefer. "I forgot to make you a mask. Sorry, Sam."

"Okay, fine," I said. "I didn't want one anyway. Dumb custom ninja masks . . . seem so cool but actually aren't . . ."

"Sam, I'm kidding," said Beefer. "Here you go, buddy." He pulled out a mask for me. It was orange and white, with felt fangs and little round ears.

"It's a Hamstersaurus Rex mask."

"Aw, man," I said as I pulled it over my face. It was kind of lumpy, but it fit okay. I was touched. "Thanks, Beefer! Okay, guys, let's—"

"Hang on! There's one more mask in here," said Beefer. He reached into his bag and pulled out a tiny piece of fabric about the size of his thumb. He handed it to me.

It was a miniature ninja mask with human eyes, ears, and hair made of felt.

"And that's a Sam mask for Hammie Rex to wear," said Beefer.

Hamstersaurus Rex shot me a look. I shrugged and gently pulled it over his head. The mask looked kind of weird on the little guy. But also kind of awesome.

We did a last-minute inventory to make sure we had the rest of our gear ready. Then all of us but Dylan grabbed an irregular parka off the rack and made a beeline for the dressing rooms.

Sure enough, just inside on the left was a door marked "Do Not Enter.'" With her Swiss Army knife, Serena jimmied the lock. We entered.

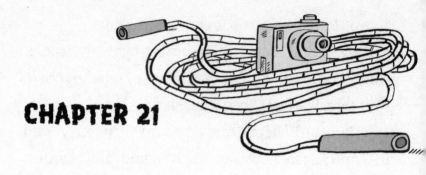

CHAPTER 21

THE DOORWAY LED into a short, dusty hall that looked like it hadn't seen much use in years. At the end of it was another door, stained with rust. According to the blueprints, this one opened right onto the ground floor of RaddZone.

I took out a pair of Serena's earphones—styled as little sparkly gargoyles—and put one in my ear.

"That's a decent mid-price pair of 'buds," said Serena. "Not gonna lie, with the XD-58s, you're going to lose a little in the bass range, but over-all a pretty bright sound. I think you'll be quite pleased with the fidelity."

"Cool?" I said.

I plugged the earphones into the jack in Beefer's walkie-talkie and held down the Talk button. "Um. Hi?" I whispered. "What's up?"

"Try not to get your thumb grease all over it," whispered Beefer.

From inside my pocket, Hammie Rex grunted at him.

The walkie-talkie crackled. "Hi, Sam," said Dylan. "Just chilling inside this coat rack. You?"

"We're about to enter RaddZone," I said. "Let me turn the camera on." I pulled my UltraLite SmartShot camera out of my bag. In night vision mode, it showed the dim hallway in a palette of glowing greens. I turned on its wireless capability and panned around. "You getting this, Dylan?"

"One sec," said Dylan. "Yep. I'm looking at the laptop and I see what you're seeing. Neat!"

"Okay, the feed is up," I said to everyone. "We're good to go."

"Commence Operation Sightless Snake," said Martha.

Martha pulled a coiled jump rope out of her backpack. She held the plastic handle at one end and handed me the other. Beefer and Serena both grabbed on to the middle of the rope.

"Blindfolds on," said Martha.

Each of us tied a bandana over our eyes. The world was pitch-black now. Totally disorienting.

"Can anybody see anything?" said Serena.

"Nope," I said. "But I can still smell Beefer."

"Who said that?" said Beefer.

"Ow! Don't step on my foot!" said Martha.

"Sorry," said Beefer. "Agh! Something hairy touched my neck!"

Serena snickered. "Just messing with you, man."

"Stop it!" said Beefer. "Not cool!"

"Shhh!" said Martha. "Listen."

"Don't worry, it wasn't a *poisonous* scorpion," said Serena.

"Wait? How do you know?" said Beefer.

"I think I hear police sirens," said Martha.

"That's just my squeaky shoe," I said. "All right, everybody: forward march!"

We awkwardly shuffled forward through the door. Holding on to the jump rope, we *were* like a blind snake; I was the head and Martha was the tail. Except we weren't exactly blind. With my other hand, I held my digital camera out in front of me, which was streaming live back to the laptop in front of Dylan, who in turn was giving us directions.

"Okay," said Dylan over the walkie-talkie, "it's looking like you're just to the left of Alien Autopsy: Turbo, about twenty feet from the snack bar."

"Any sign of Cartimandua or the Mind Mole?" I whispered into the walkie-talkie as I panned the camera right and left.

"Not seeing anything," said Dylan. "No lights on. Looks pretty deserted."

"Then let's start searching," I said. I tugged the

jump rope twice: the mutually agreed-upon silent signal for "move forward."

And so we slowly started to wind our way through RaddZone with Dylan as our eyes, guiding us forward and warning us of obstacles. Four blindfolded kids holding a jump rope wasn't the most efficient way to move—I banged my shins approximately seventy-eight times between the door and the Muscle Meter—but this way we couldn't get mind-moled.

We'd covered a couple hundred feet when Dylan came back over the walkie-talkie. "Guys, wait!" said Dylan. "I see someone. They're coming your way."

I froze. Hammie grunted. Serena bumped into me. Then Beefer. Then Martha. The four of us nearly toppled over. I whipped the camera around.

"Is it the Mind Mole?" I whispered into the walkie-talkie. "Is it Gordon Renfro?"

"Too far away. Can't tell," said Dylan. "But they're headed your way!"

"Guys, somebody's coming," I whispered to the rest of the group.

"What do we do?" said Serena.

"Execute Maneuver 72B," said Martha.

"Refresh my memory," said Serena. "What maneuver is that?"

"Is it doing a cartwheel?" said Beefer. "I hope it's doing a cartwheel!"

"Did any of you *read* the mission handouts I gave you?" said Martha.

We all mumbled excuses.

"It means hide!" said Martha.

The four of us scattered for hiding spots. You never think about it, but when you're blindfolded, hiding is almost impossible: If you can't see, how do you know if you can't be seen? It was like something out of Coach Weekes's old meditation tapes.

I was thinking this as I climbed under what I believed to be a pinball machine and smacked my head pretty hard. I stifled a yelp, but the UltraLite SmartShot slipped from my fingertips and clattered across the floor.

"Sam, what am I looking at?" said Dylan. "Why does it seem like you're under a particularly gum-encrusted foosball table?"

"Sorry!" I whispered into the walkie-talkie. "I dropped the camera! And I obviously can't see where it went!"

Still blindfolded, I groped around for it. The floor was super gross on my fingertips: years of spilled soda and RaddSpudd toppings. I didn't find my UltraLite SmartShot. But I did find something wet and something hairy. Blech.

Just then I heard footsteps. I froze. Hammie Rex squirmed in my pocket. The little guy was amped up and raring to go. I put a hand on him to calm him. Sure enough, the footsteps were slowly approaching. I held my breath. They got louder . . . and louder. They stopped right beside me.

The footsteps continued on. I breathed a sigh of relief.

Martha shrieked. I yanked off my blindfold and tossed it away.

"Help me!" cried Martha.

I scrambled out from under the pinball machine and saw Martha backing away from . . . Grumpy Grampy Gopher.

"Give us the PaleoGro!" squealed Grumpy

Grampy, who I realized now was someone in another Country Gopher mask. He wore the striped polo shirt of a RaddZone employee. "We told you to bring the hamster! Where is he?"

"Which hamster?" said Martha, her voice trembling. "Personally, I know multiple hamsters."

"You think this is a game?" screeched Grumpy Grampy. "We are not amused!" He lunged toward Martha and grabbed her with both arms.

"Oh, we brought the hamster, all right!" I said. "Chomp 'im, boy!" Hammie Rex launched out of my pocket and bounded toward Grumpy Grampy. With a flying, slobbery dino-bite, he snapped onto his forearm.

"Aaaagh!" grunted Grumpy Grampy, stumbling backward and flailing.

"Way to go, Spikehead!" cried Serena.

"Ninja jump rope attack!" cried Beefer as he and Serena ran at Grumpy Grampy, holding the rope low between them. They swept his legs out from under him and he hit the ground. A second later, Beefer and Serena were on top of him, trying to hold him down and wind the rope around his arms.

"You think you can defeat us with mere . . . jumping ropes? Risible!" cackled Grumpy Grampy as he struggled violently. "You are all but grubs compared to us!"

Hammie snorted at him.

"Snort all you want, fool. Your time is at an end!" cried Grumpy Grampy. "*We shall relish your particular doom!*" One of his arms broke free. Beefer jumped on it and squashed it to the ground. The commotion echoed throughout RaddZone.

"What do we do?" I said.

"I don't know!" said Serena. "I don't think we can hold him for too much longer!"

"I have an idea!" said Martha. She got close to Grumpy Grampy's face and stared right into the eyeholes of his rubber mask. She whipped something shiny out of her pocket. It was an old-fashioned watch on a chain. "Okay, uh, I want you to relax."

"Do we look relaxed?" squealed Grumpy Grampy.

"Focus on the sound of my voice," said Martha, swinging the pocket watch back and forth in front of his eyes. She glanced down at his name tag on his shirt, which said "Jason." "Imagine you're in a very calming, safe place, Jason. Maybe a hammock?"

"We will not!" shrieked Grumpy Grampy. "Hammocks are for the weak!"

"What's she doing?" said Serena.

"I think she's hypnotizing him," I said.

"But he's already hypnotized!" said Beefer.

"Then she's double-hypnotizing him," I said. "Or maybe unhypnotizing him?"

"Every muscle is starting to loosen," said Martha. "The tension is leaving your body."

"Lies!" squealed Grumpy Grampy. "All lies! We are extremely tense!"

"Your breathing is slowing down!" said Martha. "I'm going to count backward from forty-seven—"

"Is there any way you can hurry it up, Martha?" I said. "We don't have much time!"

"But this is how I learned it at Magician Camp," said Martha.

"Just try!"

Martha turned back to Grumpy Grampy, still swinging her watch. "Okay, I'm going to count backward from, let's say, eleven, and when I reach one, the Mind Mole's stranglehold on your psyche is going to be broken. Do you understand me, Jason? When I utter the phrase 'Advanced Placement,' you will awaken, clearheaded and free from all mental control."

"We will not!" said Grumpy Grampy. "We will crush you like beetle larvae!"

"Eleven . . . ten . . . nine," said Martha.

"You cannot hope to counter our power, you unctuous goody-goody!"

"Eight . . . seven . . . six . . ."

"You trifle with dangerous forces beyond your ken!"

"Five . . . four . . . three . . ."

"We will destroy yooooooooou!"

"Two . . . one," said Martha. "Advanced Place-ment!"

Instantly, Grumpy Grampy stopped struggling. Beefer and Serena relaxed their hold. Martha and I looked at each other.

". . . Um," said Grumpy Grampy quietly. "What's, like, happening or whatever?"

Martha put her watch back in her pocket. Serena pulled the rubber mask off. It was the floppy-haired teen who ran the RaddZone racetrack.

"Hate to tell you, guy, but you got mind-controlled by an evil mutant mole," said Serena.

"Um, okay," said Jason. "Why are you all wearing ninja masks?"

"Somehow that's even harder to explain," said Serena. "Beefer?"

"They look cool," said Beefer with a shrug.

Jason blinked. He looked like he was either going to start crying or like his floppy-haired head would explode.

"Or, you know what?" said Serena. "Maybe this is aaaaalllll a dreeeeeam."

"It is?" said Jason with a flip of his bangs. "That would be so *lame*."

I gave Martha a high five. She didn't appear to have ever received one before.

"You broke the Mind Mole's control!" I said.

"Huh, yeah, I guess I did," said Martha.

"Maybe now we can save Cartima—"

BZZZHT! A familiar electrical crackle rang out

through RaddZone. All at once, the lights flickered back on. The arcade machines and games began to play their songs and ring their bells and make their bleeps and bloops and flash every color of the rainbow all at once. The power was back on. And the normal cacophony of RaddZone filled the air.

Hamstersaurus Rex gave a low growl.

"What are you worried about, little guy?" I asked.

"Them," said Serena, looking past me.

Six masked figures surrounded us—Gomer, Big Virgil, Sweetie Pie, Dweasel, Leisl, and Aunt Ellie Mae—the rest of the Country Gopher Family!

"Who are they?" whispered Martha in horror.

"We are the Mind Mole," said the Country Gophers in eerie unison.

CHAPTER 22

"**U**M, MS. RADDENBACH," said Jason, "why are you, like, wearing a Sweetie Pie mask from the prize counter?"

"Flee, you fool," said the Country Gophers. "You are useless to us now!"

"Yes, ma'am," said Jason, and he leaped to his feet and ran for his life.

It was just us and the Country Gopher Family now. And they really didn't look like they were in the mood for a jamboree. Hamstersaurus Rex let out a ferocious roar that shook the ground.

"You've brought us the hamster, yet that was only half the bargain," said the Country Gophers,

circling around us. "We still hold Cartimandua captive in our alpine fastness. Give us the
PaleoGro!"

"You want it, Mind Mole?" said Serena. "Here
it is." She pulled the PaleoGro canister out of her
messenger bag and held it up.

The Country Gophers moved toward her.

"Or is this it?" said Beefer as he pulled an iden-
tical canister out of his backpack and twirled it on
his fingertip.

The Country Gophers hesitated.

"Or maybe this," said Martha, holding up
another.

"Nah, it's got to be this one," I said, waggling
mine. Martha's label maker had allowed us to
make perfect decoys for the real canister.

"Maneuver 181C-4!" cried Martha.

We stared at her.

"Scatter!" she said.

Each of us took off at top speed in a different
direction.

"Halt!" cried the Country Gophers. "Do not flee
from the Mind Mole!"

We didn't listen.

Serena ran for the racetrack. She hopped the barrier and got into kart number twelve.

"C'mon, start! Start!" cried Serena as Sweetie Pie clambered over the wall after her. With a squeal of the tires, Serena sped off, leaving Sweetie Pie in the dust behind her.

Martha dashed for the ball pits.

"We're coming for you, Cartimandua!" she cried. With a huge leap she dove into the extra-deep one and disappeared under the colored balls, a bit like a mole herself. Dweasel and Leisl Gopher waded in after her. I desperately hoped she would be okay.

Beefer squared off against Aunt Ellie Mae. He tucked his canister into his belt and put up his dukes. Wait, how could that be? He wasn't wearing a belt— No, he was! It was his fabled karate clear belt!

"Time to fight gopher with gopher!" cried Beefer as he assumed an odd fighting stance: both hands pulled up close to his chest while he did chewing motions with his mouth. "Gopher style!"

I made a mad dash past the claw machines before I smacked right into Big Virgil Gopher, a barrel-chested kid who had to be at least fifteen. He wrapped a beefy arm around my neck and put me in an unbreakable headlock.

"A mildly clever diversion," said Big Virgil as he ripped the PaleoGro canister from my grasp. "But in the end we will prevail. For we are the Mind—OOF!"

Hamstersaurus Rex head-butted him hard in the solar plexus, knocking the wind out of his lungs. I wriggled out of his grasp, scooped up Hammie, and scrambled around the corner toward the snack bar. I dove behind a trash can overflowing with crumpled red-foil RaddSpudd wrappers.

A few seconds later, Big Virgil lumbered past, still searching for us. "You won't get far!" he shrieked as he continued on. "The Mind Mole knows all!"

I waited till he was out of sight before I made a move.

"Dylan, you still there?" I whispered into the walkie-talkie.

I heard a crackle. "Still here," said Dylan. "Is everyone okay?"

"Not sure, but we created one heck of a diversion," I said. "The Mind Mole said he has Cartimandua in his 'alpine fastness.' Do you know what that means?"

"Honestly, that's more of a Martha question," said Dylan, "but I think it's like a mountain hideout."

"Mountain hideout?" I said. "Mount Putta-Putta!" I gazed up at the fake volcano, looming ominously over RaddZone as it trailed fake smoke into the air.

"But the Mind Mole will be expecting you," said Dylan. "There's only one way up to the top."

"Maybe there isn't," I said. "Can you take a look at the blueprints?"

"One sec," said Dylan. "Yeah, you're right! There's a maintenance ladder around the back, so they can refill the dry ice tanks! I can guide you there."

"Awesome," I said. "Over and out."

I turned to see Hamstersaurus Rex pawing the floor.

"All right, dude, this is it. The final showdown," I said. "Seems like the Mind Mole is focused on you. Maybe we can use that somehow."

Hammie Rex jumped up and down and stamped his little dino-feet. He was ready.

"Time to save Cartimandua and stop the Mind Mole, once and for all."

Hammie Rex snarled and kicked a wadded-up ball of RaddSpudd foil. As it bounced across the floor, I had an epiphany.

CHAPTER 23

HAMMIE AND I climbed the long maintenance ladder on the far side of Mount Putta-Putta. By the time we reached the top, I was covered in sweat. Now we crept close to the lip of the crater—me on all fours, Hammie on his tiptoes—for a better look.

"Wha—happe—g?" crackled Dylan in my earphone. "What—see?"

"Dylan, you're breaking up," I said. "Can you hear me? Dylan?"

"—hear—I'm n—"

"What?" I said. "Dylan, are you there?" All I heard was static. I'd lost the signal.

I was right about the Mind Mole, though. He'd made his lair on the ninth hole of the mini-golf course, in the crater at the top of the volcano. And he'd definitely done some redecorating. In a makeshift laboratory in the corner, Gordon Renfro furiously mixed bubbling chemicals. Could he be preparing the Mind Mole's dino-power concoction, ready to add PaleoGro as its final ingredient?

I shuddered as I saw the Mind Mole himself. He lounged on a throne of stuffed penguins, still wearing his tiny purple cape. With his little paws he casually gestured toward Renfro, manipulating his movements like he was conducting an orchestra that bored him.

To his left was a plate. On it was a RaddSpudd covered with thin strips of bacon that seemed to be . . . moving? No, it wasn't bacon at all. His baked potato was loaded

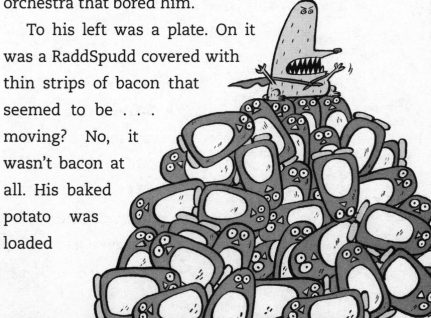

with earthworms! The Mind Mole took a big bite. I nearly threw up.

At the Mind Mole's stumpy right paw, I noticed a power switch that was connected by a coiling wire to the Country Gopher Family Jamboree—he'd somehow moved the entire animatronic stage up to the top of the fake mountain!

I gasped when I spotted Cartimandua. She was tied up to Gomer Gopher's snare drum. Was she already dead? No, just napping. But she was hardly safe. The drumstick Gomer Gopher usually held in his raised paw had been replaced with the oversized mallet from the Muscle Meter.

The Mind Mole's devilish design became apparent: one flick of that power switch beside him, the mallet would come down and crush Cartimandua!

It was good that Hamstersaurus Rex didn't go catatonic at the sight of her.

He gave a

growl of anguish instead.

"Hammie, shhh!" I said.

But it was too late. Gordon Renfro froze, and he and the Mind Mole simultaneously turned to look in our direction. I ducked back behind the lip of the crater.

"Ah, Hamstersaurus Rex. So you've made it to the proverbial mountaintop?" called out Gordon Renfro in a snide, squeaky voice. The Mind Mole was speaking through him now. "Our noble hero who's *sooooo* special, whom all the kid-dies adore *sooooo* much. Why don't you come out of there where we can get a good look at you?"

"No chance, Mind Mole!" I yelled back. "I'll give you the PaleoGro and you can let Cartimandua go. I brought Hamstersaurus Rex to 'bear witness' like you said. That was the deal."

I held the PaleoGro canister up over the lip of the volcano. I felt that staticky sensation right before it was ripped out of my hand by the unseen power of the Mind Mole's telekinesis.

I heard the sound of Gordon Renfro opening it. He snorted. "This is baking soda with green food coloring in it. We won't ask again. The PaleoGro. Now. Or Cartimandua meets her ignominious end as so much hamster goo!"

I didn't want to do it. But what choice did I have? Hammie looked like he was in agony. It was all I could do to hold him back from charging in to save her—a move that would probably get him killed, too. I reached deep into the inside pocket of my backpack and pulled out a second PaleoGro canister. The real one.

"If I give it to you, you'll release her?" I cried.

"We are a mole of our word," said Renfro. "We will release Cartimandua."

I held it up. Once again the canister flew from my fingertips. I heard a chemical whoosh. Again I risked a peek over the lip of the volcano to see that Gordon Renfro had dumped all of the PaleoGro into his bubbling concoction. Instantly it turned from a dull gray to a bright foamy purple.

Renfro cackled as he removed the beaker full of purple sludge from its burner. "You didn't let us finish," he said. "We will release Cartimandua *right after Hamstersaurus Rex drinks this*."

On his throne, the Mind Mole clapped his grubby little paws together in smug satisfaction.

"Huh?" I said. "Why would Hamstersaurus drink it? I thought you wanted the PaleoGro to give yourself dino-powers!"

"Oh no," giggled Renfro. "How laughably crude. The thought never crossed our brilliant mind."

"Well, what is that stuff, then? Some kind of poison?" I yelled back. "No way Hamstersaurus Rex is drinking that!"

"Not poison," said Gordon Renfro. "It is an antidote of sorts. This formula will turn Hamstersaurus Rex back into a regular hamster."

CHAPTER 24

THE MIND MOLE now stood upon his plush penguin throne, his cape flapping behind him. Closer to me, Gordon Renfro spoke his words: "You know we and Hamstersaurus Rex come from the same laboratory. Indeed, this makes us brothers of a sort."

"Guess Hammie got the looks, huh?" I yelled back.

The Mind Mole continued unfazed: "Both of us rodents; both human-made freaks of nature. Yet the more I studied him, the more I realized our lives couldn't have turned out more differently. I was kept by scientists in darkness and solitude, while he was cheered on by smiling schoolchildren. His mutation inspires adoration, whereas mine inspires only hatred and contempt. I am despised and he is loved. How is this fair?"

"You act like a creep. You use people like puppets. Oh, and your little cape looks stupid!" I yelled back. "Maybe that's why you're not exactly Mr. Popularity?"

"Hamstersaurus Rex is only special, only interesting, only a hero, because he's half dinosaur. Take away the '-saurus Rex' and he's nothing. Less than nothing! No one will care."

"Hmm. It sounds like you're kind of obsessed with him," I called back.

"AM NOT!" screeched Renfro. I'd finally gotten under the Mind Mole's skin.

"That's why you took all those creepy stalker photos," I said. "That's why you had superhero comics and *How to Not Be Unlikable* in your weird little hidey-hole. You're crazy jealous of Hammie Rex! Sounds pretty unhealthy, if you ask me."

"SILENCE!" cried Renfro. "WE HOLD CARTIMANDUA'S LIFE IN OUR VERY CLAWS! YOU HAVE

TEN SECONDS TO DECIDE! TEN . . ."

The Mind Mole put his paw on the power switch. I didn't have long to weigh my options.

I held down the Talk button of the walkie-talkie. "Dylan, help!" I said. "The Mind Mole wants to take Hamstersaurus Rex's powers away! What should I do?" I listened. Nothing. Just static.

Renfro continued counting. "Nine . . . eight . . . seven . . ."

I peeked over the lip of the crater again. Cartimandua was about thirty feet away. There was no way I could make it to her before the Mind Mole could flick that switch and Gomer's mallet came down. Even Hammie Rex couldn't cover the distance that fast.

"Six . . . five . . . four . . ."

"Okay, okay!" I cried. "It's up to him, though. It's Hammie's choice whether or not he drinks your stupid formula."

I turned to look at Hamstersaurus Rex. He stared back at me.

"Look, dude, I don't know if you can understand me or not, but that jerk of a mole wants you to drink that nasty purple ooze and give up your dinosaur powers," I said. "Unless we do something, Cartimandua has about three seconds to live. It's up to you, I guess. I can't tell you what to do."

Hammie Rex licked his lips. He seemed to be mulling it over. With a grunt, the little guy scrambled over the lip of the volcano and down into the crater. He'd made his choice.

Hamstersaurus Rex stood at Gordon Renfro's feet and opened his dino-jaws wide. The Mind Mole rubbed his paws together with glee.

"Down the hatch, *dear brother*," said Gordon Renfro, and he poured the entire potion down Hamstersaurus Rex's throat.

For an instant, nothing happened. I allowed myself a glimmer of hope. Maybe it wouldn't work? Maybe the Mind Mole had somehow messed up the formula?

But he hadn't.

Hamstersaurus Rex twitched. Then he twitched again. Then he crumpled to the ground, foaming at the mouth and convulsing. He was dying!

The Mind Mole hopped up and down on his throne now, unable to contain his excitement.

"What have you done to him?" I cried, leaping over the lip of the volcano and running toward Hammie Rex. "You killed my best friend!"

"No," said Renfro, "it is a fate far worse than death. He will be *ordinary*!"

I reached Hammie's side. Sure enough, his spiky tail and fangs were gone now. His belly had no more scales. He was a normal hamster, like the kind you might buy in any pet shop. I cradled him in my hands.

"Come on. Please be okay," I whispered. "Please be okay, little guy."

Hamstersaurus Rex suddenly awakened. He looked around and gave a frightened squeak. Then he sprang out of my hands and scurried away in terror.

"Hammie, wait!" I cried.

But he'd already disappeared between two fake rocks.

The Mind Mole giggled through Gordon Renfro. "Do you see? Without his powers, he isn't brave.

He isn't noble. He isn't anything. Just a frightened little rodent! No one will love him now. I may not have killed him, but truly Hamstersaurus Rex is dead," said Renfro. "Mmmm, victory tastes sweeter than the tenderest termite larva."

Tears welled in my eyes. "He did it to help an innocent hamster!"

"Ah, yes. Thank you for reminding us," said Renfro. "Now that we have won decisively, we suppose we don't need Cartimandua anymore, do we?" The Mind Mole moved his claw toward the power switch.

"What?!" I cried. "But you promised you'd let her go!"

"We lied, of course," cackled Renfro. "Your gullibility is boundless. Perhaps there is a lesson in all this for you?"

The Mind Mole flicked the switch. There was a pop, followed by a blinding flash of light. I covered my eyes. But when I opened them, the mallet hadn't moved. Cartimandua, now awake, blinked serenely.

"What happened?" cried Renfro.

I turned and saw Hamstersaurus Rex lying on the ground, unconscious. My breath caught in my lungs. His limp body was next to the cord that connected the power switch to the Country Gopher Family Jamboree. Smoke curled upward from a spot where he'd gnawed clean through it.

"No!" cried Renfro as the Mind Mole frantically flipped the switch off and on. "No, no, no, no, no!" It still didn't work. Hamstersaurus Rex, a regular hamster, had saved Cartimandua's life.

"See?" I said. "It's not being half dinosaur that makes him special at all. He's a hero because of the choices he makes."

"SILENCE!" cried Renfro. The Mind Mole looked utterly gobsmacked.

"You want to be like him?" I said. "Maybe try helping people instead of hurting them."

"WE WILL NOT LISTEN TO ANY MORE OF THIS DRIVEL!" cried Renfro. "NO MORE! WE COMMAND YOU!"

The Mind Mole stared into my eyes. I didn't look away. They gleamed with malevolent intensity . . . those eyes . . .

Those eyes had no effect on me. I whipped out a pillowcase and lunged for the Mind Mole.

You see, while hiding behind the trash can, I'd realized that Old Man Ohlman wasn't immune to Mind Mole's mind control at all. The only difference between him and anybody else was that weird tinfoil hat of his—the hat was what blocked the Mind Mole's power! So I decided to line the inside of my ninja mask with old RaddSpudd wrappers from the trash. Was it greasy? Sure. Was my scalp going to smell weird for days, perhaps months? Obviously. But those foil wrappers had saved me!

I yanked the pillowcase down over the Mind Mole and tied it closed. From inside, the Mind Mole thrashed and squeaked in disbelief.

"How?" cried Gordon Renfro, dumbfounded. "None can resist us!"

I felt a tremor. All around me, objects started to tear themselves free of the ground—plaster rocks, life preservers, the strips of fake turf that lined the mini-golf course—and swirl up into the air. In his panic, the Mind Mole was now unleashing

the full power of his telekinesis. It was terrifying!

But his power was wild and unfocused. A conch shell shattered on the ground beside me. A beaker from Renfro's makeshift lab sailed past my face and exploded against the rim of the volcano.

"Unhand us!" cried Gordon Renfro as he charged at me through the swirling storm of debris.

"Not without Cartimandua!" I said, and broke in her direction. But I froze as the Muscle Meter mallet ripped itself from animatronic Gomer Gopher's claws and spun through the air right at my head. Somehow I managed to dive out of the way. The mallet missed me by a couple of inches.

"You cannot hope to prevail," cried Gordon Renfro. "We are the—"

KATHUNK! The flying mallet caught Gordon Renfro right in the face. It sent him tumbling over the edge of the volcano and down its slope.

Random objects shattered and burst and tore themselves to bits around me. Still clutching the pillowcase holding the weakly thrashing Mind Mole—he *was* physically pathetic—I crawled toward Cartimandua.

"Sorry I got you mixed up in all of this," I said as I untied her.

She seemed utterly unfazed by everything that had happened. Kind of bored, actually. Good for her, I guess. I tucked her into my shirt pocket and scrambled back to Hammie Rex. The little guy was hurt bad. I didn't have time to check his vitals. So I blinked back my tears, scooped him up, and tucked him delicately in my other pocket.

BOOM! A heavy plaster porpoise smashed to pieces right next to me. The ground shook, like the whole fake volcano might actually collapse. There was no way I was climbing back down the maintenance ladder while Mount Putta-Putta practically ripped itself apart. I jumped to my feet and started to run down the mountain, dodging flying projectiles all the way.

I rounded the corner of the seventh hole to see a huge figure blocking my path. My heart sank. It was Big Virgil Gopher.

"You resisted our mind control. A triflingly clever ploy, we'll grant you that," said Big Virgil in a creaky Mind Mole voice. "But we shall not be captured. Oh no, we are far too intelligent for that."

Big Virgil snatched the bag from me and shoved me to the ground.

"BEHOLD! THE MIND MOLE ESCAPES!" he cackled. Then Big Virgil turned and started to flee down the mountain. The Mind Mole was getting away, and there was nothing I could do about it!

"Not so fast!" cried someone farther down the slope.

It was Dylan! She tossed something like a grenade right into Big Virgil's path. It wasn't a grenade, though. It was an open sour cream packet.

Big Virgil's foot hit the packet and shot out from under him. He did a complete flip and landed flat on his back. The Mind Mole's pillowcase went sailing through the air and smacked against a fake palm tree with a dull thud.

Instantly all the floating objects fell to the ground. A good bump to his soft, swollen head and the Mind Mole had been knocked out cold.

"Thanks, Dylan!" I cried, giving her a massive hug.

"Sorry it took me so long," said Dylan. "Broken ankle, of course. Also I had to make a little detour along the way."

"Hamstersaurus Rex is hurt," I said. "He gnawed through an electrical wire to save Cartimandua's life."

I took the little guy out of my pocket and laid him in the cool, fake grass. He looked bad. There were scorch marks around his mouth and he wasn't moving at all. I listened but I heard no breathing.

"I think . . . he's gone," I said. I no longer held back my tears.

"Sam, there's no way a normal hamster could survive that," said Dylan. "I know there's no Paleo-Gro left, but . . . maybe these could work?"

Dylan unzipped her backpack to reveal several brightly colored containers. It took me a moment to realize what they were: Dinoblast Powerpacker.

"That's why I was late," said Dylan. "Had to hobble next door to Harry's Health Food Hut to buy these." She tossed me a container of Power-packer.

I popped the lid off and dipped the tip of my pinkie finger into the powder. Then I held it to Hamstersaurus Rex's mouth. Nothing.

"Come on, Hammie," I whispered. "Come on . . . Come on . . ."

The little guy's pink tongue flicked out and slurped the powder off my finger. I dipped it back into the container. He licked at it again. I gave him more, and more. Soon I was practically shoveling the stuff into his mouth by the handful. His little paws begin to change. A scaly tail started to sprout. . . .

CHAPTER 25

A **MIGHTY ROAR RANG** out through all of RaddZone: Hamstersaurus Rex was back! I hugged the little guy close. Even Cartimandua seemed impressed.

"Nice hamsters, bro," said Big Virgil as he pulled his mask off. I now recognized him as the big, pimply-faced teen who worked the prize counter. "Couple questions: What's going on here? What's in that pillowcase? Why does my ankle hurt? And who's that guy?"

"Long story; the Mind Mole; you slipped on sour cream," said Dylan. "And that guy is—"

"Gordon Renfro!" I cried.

Gordon Renfro crept forward, rubbing a bump on his head the size of a RaddSpudd. He was now free of the Mind Mole's control, too. He saw us staring at him.

"What are you brats gawping at?" cried Gordon Renfro as he snatched the pillowcase that held the unconscious Mind Mole inside. "This telepathic mole is the intellectual property of SmilesCorp! In fact, so is that mutant dino-hamster! I'll sue you! I'll sue all of you!"

He started toward Hamstersaurus Rex. Hammie snarled dangerously.

"Oh man, that was perfect," said Serena. She was pointing my UltraLite SmartShot right at him. Beefer and Martha stood behind her, arms crossed. "You literally said the name of the company and everything."

Gordon Renfro cocked his head. "Aren't you the little girl who hangs around and organizes our office supplies on alternate Wednesdays?"

"Nope," said Serena. "I'm an investigative journalist. And you just gave me the scoop of a lifetime."

"She's going to start a blog someday!" said Beefer.

"By the way, I found your camera, Sam," said Serena.

"Thanks," I said.

"Give me that tape," snapped Gordon Renfro.

"First of all, it's digital," I said. "Second, what are you going to do, beat up a twelve-year-old girl?"

"Please do!" said Serena, still filming. "That would make this story even awesomer."

Gordon Renfro started toward Serena.

"It's already in the cloud, Mr. Renfro," said Martha.

Gordon Renfro paused and collected himself. I could see him thinking it through. "I mean, uh . . . no comment," he mumbled, backing away as he held the Mind Mole in the sack. "No comment."

"Hey!" I cried. "You stop right there!"

He didn't. With a parting "No comment!" he leaped over the edge of the volcano and half slid, half tumbled away down the slope.

By the time we reached the base of Mount Putta-Putta, Gordon Renfro was gone.

"Something tells me we haven't seen the last of that guy," I said.

"Forget him, Sam. The most important thing is that you saved Cartimandua," said Martha, grabbing her from me and planting little kisses all over her. Cartimandua squeaked.

"Not me," I said. "It was the little guy."

Hammie Rex hopped up and down in my hand, growling happily and slobbering everywhere.

Martha gave Hamstersaurus Rex a solemn salute. "This is unprecedented, but . . . by the power vested in me by Horace Hotwater Middle School, I hereby appoint you, Hamstersaurus Rex, to the rank of Hamster Monitor, First Class!"

"Can a hamster become a Hamster Monitor?" said Dylan.

"This one can," I said.

Dylan and I both gave Hammie Rex the same salute. Then we broke down laughing.

"What's a 'Hamster Monitor'?" asked Serena.

"Look, we'll catch you up on everything," said Beefer. "The first thing you've got to understand is that Sam used to be this horrible bully . . ."

CHAPTER 26

"**H**OME, **SWEET REINFORCED** titanium home," I said as I gently placed Cartimandua back into the PETCATRAZ Pro™ on Wednesday morning before class. She kicked up a few cedar shavings and then turned to stare at her favorite spot on the wall.

"Safe and sound," said Dylan. "Doing what she does best."

"So," said Martha, "as Hamster Monitors, how do we make sure this type of thing never, *ever* happens again?"

"How do we make sure the type of thing where Cartimandua is abducted by an evil mole with paranormal mental powers never happens again?" I said.

Martha nodded.

"Hmm," I said. "Maybe put an extra lock on the cage?"

"Or set up some sort of laser grid," said Dylan.

"I like Dylan's suggestion," said Martha.

From my pocket, Hamstersaurus Rex gave a gurgly little coo. Cartimandua shot a glance in his direction. If I were to play the highly subjective game of interpreting hamster facial expressions, I'd say she kinda-sorta smiled. Maybe. Was it true love? Or simply the beginning of a beautiful hamster friendship? Who knew? Maybe Cartimandua just wanted to get a better look at a different wall?

But I did know that Hamstersaurus Rex was back to his old happy, slobbery self again. Whatever his future held, the little guy seemed to be okay with it for the moment. I scratched him on his back spikes and he gave a contented belch.

That day at lunch I made an official announcement: after helping to rescue our new classroom hamster, I was done taking any new "cases" for the moment. My career as a boy detective was officially on ice.

"I think that's the right choice," said Tina Gomez. "You weren't very good at it anyway."

Coach Weekes intercepted me in the hall. "Gibbs! Just the kid I was looking to see. I have to know: How did things work out for your so-called wink-wink friend and his or her, but probably his, life goals?"

I didn't quite know how to answer. "Seems like . . . it is what it is."

Coach nodded sagely and put a hand on my shoulder. "You're welcome," he said. "And now, I'm off to quit my job."

"Wait!" I said. "Don't do that. We, uh, need you here at Horace Hotwater."

Coach Weekes smiled. "No, no, Gibbs. I've made up my mind," he said. "Don't try to talk me out of this decision by telling me stuff like I'm basically the heart and soul of this school, and things would completely fall apart around here without me."

"Uh. But Coach, you're the heart and soul of this school and things would completely fall apart around here without you," I said.

"You know what? You're right, Gibbs. I think I'll stay," said Coach Weekes. "Thanks for the little nudge."

After school, I collected Hammie Rex from Meeting Club HQ. Martha had cleared her entire extracurricular schedule for the afternoon and Dylan blew off disc golf practice—she was relegated to the sidelines anyway. The four of us set out across Maple Bluffs.

Our first stop was a run-down house with a shiny roof. I knocked on the door. Old Man Ohlman answered, tinfoil hat gleaming in the afternoon sun.

"Are you another sixth grader from the phone company?" he said. "I told the last one that I wasn't interested in whatever it was he was selling and I thought that would be the end of it."

"I'm the *same* sixth grader from the phone company," I said. "And I'm not from the phone company!"

Martha and Dylan gave each other a look.

"Mr. Ohlman, we just wanted to thank you," I said.

"For my service in the Franco-Prussian War?" he said.

"Sure," I said. "But also, in your own, ah, *unconventional* way, you helped us beat the bad guy and save an innocent hamster's life."

"You mean that one, right there?" said Mr. Ohlman, beaming at Hamstersaurus Rex in my pocket.

"No, a different hamster," mumbled Dylan.

"Either way," said Old Man. "Means a lot, you kids coming here to show your appreciation. It warms an old man's heart. Son, I want you to have this."

He placed a smooth ceramic object in my hand and closed my fingers around it. I took a look. It was a little bald baby with huge white muttonchops.

"That's one of my treasured Baby President figurines," said Old Man Ohlman. "It's Martin Van Buren. Our nation's *first* president."

"Actually, sir," said Martha, "that's not entirely acc—"

I waved her off. It just wasn't worth it.

"Thanks, Mr. Ohlman," I said. "I've always wanted something like . . . a small fragile figurine of an American president. But as a baby."

"That'll be three dollars, please," said Old Man Ohlman. He held out his hand.

Hammie Rex snorted. I sighed and gave him three bucks, and we continued on our way.

We headed to the Ramblewood Arms apartment building. Dylan punched the buzzer for 3F and we waited.

"That's peculiar," said Martha. "Why are there two mailboxes on the corner? I'm going to call our congressperson."

"No need," I said as I approached them. "Beefer? Is that you?" I said to the one on the left.

"BOO!" yelled the trash can beside them, practically scaring me and Hamstersaurus Rex half to death.

Martha and Dylan stifled laughter. Hammie looked like he wanted to chomp someone.

"Ha! I can't believe you were fooled by my decoy mailbox," said Beefer from inside the trash can.

"You made a whole trash can costume just to yell 'boo' at me, you maniac?" I said. My heart was still pounding.

"Yep. Took me nineteen hours. But so worth it for the look on your face, which was probably pretty great. I couldn't actually tell," said Beefer. "Kind of limited visibility in this thing."

"Okay, well, yeah, you 'got' me," I said. "And since you can't see, I'm doing air quotes."

"Seriously, Sam," said Beefer. "This is the oldest trick in the book."

"Oh, so you've finally read a book?" I said.

Upstairs, we found Serena Sandoval hunched over her computer, looking nervous. But she grinned when she saw Hamstersaurus Rex.

"Heya, Spikehead!" she cried. Hammie bounded over to her and nuzzled her hand.

"So, is it ready for publication?" said Martha.

"I think so. Maybe not? It's amazing. Could be better. Actually, it stinks," said Serena, burying her face in her hands.

"Pregame jitters. Sometimes you've just got to take a swing and see what happens," said Dylan. "Wow, I just realized how much I sound like Coach Weekes right now, so I'm gonna stop talking."

"No need to worry, Serena," I said. "Your article is fantastic."

She had composed a very long blog post describing SmilesCorp's secret Genetic Research and Development Lab, and exposing the company's role in the recent outbreak of freaky animals all over Maple Bluffs. She'd backed it up with interviews with the Mind Mole's victims and included scans of her great-aunt Sue's files. The icing on the cake was a short video clip of SmilesCorp lab chief Gordon Renfro saying, "This telepathic mole is the intellectual property of SmilesCorp! In fact, so is that mutant dino-hamster!" Martha had even double-checked it for grammar.

The only thing left to do was to click "Publish," which, after much coaxing, Serena agreed to do. She let Hammie Rex step on the mouse.

"Guess I made my journalistic debut," said Serena. "Kind of thought it would be music criticism, but you've got to start somewhere."

"SmilesCorp won't know what hit them," I said. "Now all we have to do is sit back and wait."

We sat back. We waited. We all looked at one another. Hammie Rex chewed on his own foot.

"Guys, am I crazy, or are we all thinking the same thing?" said Beefer.

"RaddZone!" Dylan, Serena, Beefer, and I said in unison.

"No votes for the Antique Doll Museum?" said Martha. "Fine, okay, let's go to RaddZone."

And we did. And it was awesome.

MORE BOOKS IN THE
HAMSTERSAURUS REX SERIES!

Beware: Rampaging mutant dino-hamster!